Dear Readers,

Mistletoe and holly, carols and cookies—and *so* many gifts to shop for! Escape the season's stress with four Bouquet romances guaranteed to restore your goodwill . . . and renew your faith in love.

Scandal and suspense are the name of the game in popular author Jona Jeffrey's Bouquet debut, **Seducing Tony,** when a woman sets out to find the man she believes ruined her father . . . and discovers that passion is much sweeter than revenge. In **Mountain Moonlight,** by talented author Jane Anderson, a single mother's camping trip with her young son becomes a nostalgic journey into her past when her guide turns out to be the one man she could never forget.

But second chances at love aren't always easy. Beloved Silhouette and Loveswept author Suzanne McMinn proves it in **Every Breath You Take,** reuniting a couple whose painful breakup broke both their hearts—but now they must uncover a dangerous criminal before their new chance at happiness is threatened. Finally, first-time Bouquet author Cindy Hillyer sets off **Fireworks** with her tale of two independent single parents asked to plan a kindergarten picnic—only to discover that when they're together the sparks really fly.

So take a few minutes away from the holiday crush to give yourself a gift . . . four captivating love stories from Bouquet.

The Editors

MOON MAGIC

Vala watched Bram lay the ground sheet on a flat area by the tent opening. He unrolled his sleeping bag; then, holding hers, he glanced at her with one eyebrow raised. Damn the man, he was leaving the choice up to her—in the tent alone or out here with the stars and the moon. And him.

She hesitated, then nodded. Why deny what she wanted? If this night together would be all they ever had, why turn down the chance to have this much?

As he rolled out her sleeping bag next to his, her breath caught. Would she regret her decision?

"Found the Big Dipper yet?" Bram said from close beside her.

Lost in her thoughts, she hadn't heard him approach. "What?" she stammered. "Uh, no. Where is it?"

He put his arm around her shoulders and pointed at the sky. When she leaned her head back to look up it rested against him. Warmth tingled through her, and she gazed at the seven stars.

"Remember which two of them point to the North Star?" he asked.

Leaning against him, breathing in his masculine scent, she couldn't get her mind to focus. "I used to know," she said finally, looking at him instead of at the sky.

He glanced down at her, his eyes turned mysterious by the moon, holding a glint of that silvery light in them. Making a sound very like a growl low in his throat, he pulled her to him and covered her mouth with his. Her lips parted in welcome and the moon, the stars, and the mountain vanished—everything but Bram.

MOUNTAIN MOONLIGHT

JANE ANDERSON

Zebra Books
Kensington Publishing Corp.
http://www.zebrabooks.com

ZEBRA BOOKS are published by

Kensington Publishing Corp.
850 Third Avenue
New York, NY 10022

First Printing: December, 1999
10 9 8 7 6 5 4 3 2 1

Printed in the United States of America

PROLOGUE

Vala Channing watched the old man hobble from his room to stand in the hallway. She didn't have to glance at her watch to know it was three-thirty, give or take a minute or two. Though John Mokesh's dark eyes, deeply set in his wrinkled brown face, could no longer see well enough to read the time on the largest clock, he seemed to have a sixth sense about anything that mattered to him.

When the school bus stopped outside Hudson Heights Convalescent Hospital, Mr. Mokesh was always waiting in the hall, peering toward the wing entrance, ready to greet Davis. The friendship between her nine-year-old son and the ninety-four-year-old no longer bothered Vala, even though she sometimes worried that Davis didn't seem to have any friends other than John Mokesh.

Minutes later Davis appeared at the far end of the hall. Her heart lifted, as usual, when she saw her son and at the same time ached for him. He was small for his age and slight and he wore glasses. He didn't mind the glasses so much but he hated being the shortest boy in his grade.

"There's even girls bigger than me," he'd complained last year.

This year he hadn't complained at all. Instead he'd withdrawn—even from her.

Vala waved at him and forced herself to turn away to go back to her office, knowing Davis preferred the company of John Mokesh to hers. Since she was at work, it was just as well—or so she told herself. The hospital paid her to be their social worker, not to spend working hours with her son. It wasn't easy being a single parent and she was grateful her employer had agreed to allow Davis to come to the hospital to spend the two hours between the end of his school day and the time she finished work.

Since Mr. Mokesh rarely spoke to any of the hospital employees and Davis had been unusually quiet this past year, she sometimes wondered what on earth the two of them found to say to each other. . . .

In Mokesh's room, Davis tossed his bookbag on the bed and shrugged out of his winter jacket, giving his friend time to hobble back inside and lower himself into a chair.

"I smell snow in the air you bring inside with you," Mokesh said.

His mother said he had to say Mr. Mokesh but

the old man wouldn't let him. "Mokesh is what I'm called," he'd told Davis. "It's an old name, a good name among my people. I don't need or want any mister."

"It's cold enough to snow," Davis agreed as he pulled up the other chair to sit near Mokesh. "Maybe we'll have snow on the ground for Christmas."

"Before you leave today I have a gift for you." The old man said. "This gift comes from long-ago ancestors. It's something to be passed on only to one who'll use the gift in the proper way. You're not Ndee but your heart is the right kind. You'll know what to do."

Davis knew Ndee was the word Mokesh's people called themselves, instead of Apache. "Apache is an enemy name for us. Why should we use it?" he'd asked. Davis also knew that Mokesh had no living relatives left.

"I'll do my best," he promised, wondering what Mokesh intended to give him. There was no point in asking his friend what the gift was or how he was supposed to use it because after months of friendship with Mokesh he was well aware of what the answer would be.

You'll know when the time comes.

"It'll be strange to die so far from the land of my birth," Mokesh said. "But no stranger than living here has been." He nodded at Davis. "When I met you, I understood why my journey brought me to this place in New York and stranded me here."

Davis was still focused on the word "die." He swallowed and said, "Are you sick?"

Mokesh shrugged. "My time has come to die."

"But—but you can't know that!" Davis sputtered in protest.

"I'm Ndee. I know. Don't be upset. I'm not."

Davis blinked back the tears that threatened. "But you're my friend."

Mokesh nodded. "I'll tell you a story about Dream Woman, about how the Ndee got their name."

Davis wanted to protest some more but held his tongue and waited. Mokesh's Ndee tales were his way of explaining things. While Davis sometimes didn't completely understand what the old man meant, the stories fascinated him. They weren't simple and easy to grasp like those he saw on TV but they stayed in his mind. Sometimes at night when he couldn't go to sleep right away, he liked to think about Mokesh's stories.

Still, he wasn't convinced any story in the world could explain to him why Mokesh had to die. What was he going to do if Mokesh really did die? He'd lose his best friend. His only friend.

"This is also a story about how to control fear," Mokesh said and paused.

Control fear? Davis wondered. "Do you mean conquer fear?" he asked.

Mokesh shook his head. "Fear is an enemy that never be defeated. Fear always survives. The an can do is learn how to control fear instead of allowing it to control him. And this is a hard lesson."

As he waited for Mokesh to begin the story, Davis tried to figure out what controlling fear had to do with losing a friend. Not much, he decided.

He wanted to reach for the old man's hand, hang onto him and never let him go, but he didn't. He'd already learned that along with not being able to make certain people love you or even like you, there was no way you could keep anyone with you by force or by pleas.

Except for his mom, it looked like he was going to be alone all over again. A real bummer, and he didn't think the story he was about to hear was going to help make it any better.

"Don't die," he begged the old man, unable to help himself.

Mokesh touched him on the shoulder. "Listen to the story. It will stay with you when I'm gone. That's what stories are for. To teach and also to comfort. Remember, only the sun and the moon and the stars and the earth last. Everything else has a time and then is gone. Your time has just begun, while mine is over. Yet I will still live in your memory of my stories. That is always the way."

ONE

"Apache Junction," Davis said as Vala stopped the rental car in front of a store advertising camping equipment. "That's a really cool name for a town, Mom."

Seeing his enthusiasm made her almost forget the hassle of getting here—how she'd argued and pleaded for ten days off so they could fly to Arizona after the Christmas holidays, which she knew she couldn't take off. Davis would have to miss a week or so of school, but that couldn't be helped. Finally her employer had begrudgingly given her the seven vacation days she had coming plus another three-day leave of absence.

She was grateful she hadn't been fired. Heaven knows she needed the job. Since Neal's new wife had blessed him with a son last May, he tended to be careless about his child support payments for Davis. He was equally careless about keeping in touch with his firstborn son. Or maybe heartless was the right word.

Davis tugged at her arm. "Look!" He pointed. "That's it—that's Superstition Mountain."

She stared at the towering mass of rock—volcanic, she'd read somewhere—off to the northeast. It wasn't her first view of the mountain because she'd lived in Phoenix when she was young. Her thought now was the same as she'd had back then—Superstition Mountain didn't look real, thrusting up forbiddingly as it did in the middle of this flat land.

"I'm glad we came," Davis said, his gaze fixed on the mountain. "Really, really glad."

So was she. Davis probably believed he'd convinced her to make the trip because of his earnest arguments about how finding the treasure was going to make up for having to spend a lot of money to get to Arizona. She didn't intend to admit to her son that she was willing to do anything to keep the bright glow of enthusiasm in his eyes. Before John Mokesh gave him the old deerskin map, Davis hadn't been interested in anything. Even his Christmas computer game, one he wanted, failed to fill the bill.

Poor Mr. Mokesh had died in his sleep the night after he'd presented Davis with the map. To her surprise, her son had accepted the old man's death without excessive grief, saying, "Mokesh told me it was his time to die. That's why he gave me his treasure map."

"Mom, you're lollygagging," Davis said. The word came from her father and probably from his father, but it had caught Davis's attention and he liked to use it.

"I was just thinking," she said.

He grabbed her hand, tugging her toward the store entrance. Once inside, Vala told the clerk, a tanned, healthy-looking woman with a long braid down her back, that she and her son planned to make a trip into the Superstitions. "But I don't know much about camping," she admitted, "and so I haven't the faintest idea what we'll need."

The clerk's eyebrows raised. "You're planning to trek into the Superstitions without knowing anything about camping? I hate to rain on your parade but that is *not* a good idea. Not without a guide. That mountain isn't greenhorn-friendly. Fact is, Superstition Mountain can't be called friendly to *anyone*."

"A guide?" Vala repeated. "How do I go about finding one?" She hadn't planned on any extra expenses, but maybe guides took credit cards.

"We got a list posted." The woman jerked a thumb toward a bulletin board near the front of the store. "Names and phone numbers. We don't guarantee any of the guides but, as far as we've heard, they're all able to bring you out of the Superstitions in almost as good a shape as you were when you went in. Any one of them can tell you what you need to buy and we'll be more than glad to sell you whatever they recommend."

Thanking her, Vala went to take a look at the

list while Davis roamed through the store, examining the camping gear.

The third name on the guide list was crossed off. Perversely, she wondered why, leaning closer to see if she could make out the letters beneath the heavy dark line. Was it Bruce something? Or Brian? No, that was an "a" and then an "m" after the Br. She gasped, staring at the paper in disbelief. Bram! Was it possible? The last name certainly looked like Hunter.

Turning toward the clerk, she called, "What about this Bram Hunter? Why is he crossed off?"

The woman shrugged. "That's Bram for you. He only works when he feels like it."

Glancing at the list again, Vala took a pen from her bag and squinted at the paper as she wrote down the barely legible phone number, all the time telling herself it was a waste of time. Bram had taken his name off the list, so why call him? She already knew he wasn't available as a guide, and if she made the call for old times' sake, he probably wouldn't remember her. Why should he? She'd left Phoenix with her family when she was sixteen and, at that age, she'd been a bookish, mousy, overly shy girl.

He might not remember her, but she'd never quite forgotten him. At eighteen Bram Hunter was the most handsome boy in the school, with just enough of a shadowed reputation to intrigue every girl she knew. Including her. Her mother, unlike the mothers of her friends, had never bothered to warn her to steer clear of Bram Hunter, believing Vala was too shy to speak to *any* boy.

Her mother had been right—in a way. But there were some things her mother never found out.

Is it possible Bram recalls that night with the same awful clarity that I do? Vala wondered.

Bram Hunter lounged on his terrace, gazing at Camelback Mountain, absently stroking Sheba, the Siamese draped across his lap. The day was warm and sunny, no more than Phoenix deserved after a week of rain. He hoped the good weather held until Friday when he'd be leaving for the Caribbean.

A squeak from the depths of the house roused the Siamese and she leaped off his lap to hurry inside to her five tiny kittens.

Motherhood had certainly changed Sheba's personality—tied to her kittens, she'd actually become a worrier. He hoped she'd regain her zany, carefree attitude once her brood was old enough to leave for homes of their own. He'd made mistakes in his life but luckily none of them had been the mistake of tying himself down to a wife and family.

Marriage had never been on his agenda. He yawned and settled back on the lounge. In less than a week he'd be scuba diving off St. Amaris, one of the islands the tourists hadn't yet found. He hated crowds. He wouldn't mind a stray blonde or two to spice up the night life, though, the kind of woman who wasn't looking for any real involvement, just a few laughs. He smiled and closed his eyes.

The phone rang, jolting him. Muttering a curse, he rose and padded into the house, aware he'd left the answering machine turned off.

"Hunter," he growled into the phone.

"Uh, hello," a woman said. "This is Bram Hunter, isn't it?" He didn't recognize her voice.

He grunted an assent. When she didn't immediately continue, he said impatiently, "What was it you wanted?"

"I was wondering if you—that is, do you remember me?"

Bram rolled his eyes. Guessing games. He hated cutesy. "How the hell do I know?"

There was a pause and then she said, "I'm Vala Channing."

Vala. For a long moment he forgot to breathe. She was the last person in the world he'd ever expected to hear from. "Yes," he said finally. "I remember you."

"I wasn't sure you would. I'm in Apache Junction and I happened to see your name on a guide list."

He frowned. "I thought I took my name off that list."

"Well, it *was* crossed off."

After another pause, he said, "Are you living in Arizona now?"

"No. Davis and I—he's my son—are just visiting here."

So she was married. "Your husband's not with you?"

"I'm divorced."

I'm, not we're. Most people said *we're* divorced. Was that significant? Bram shook his head. Why should he care how she worded it?

"I was wondering," she added, then paused again.

Evidently Vala hadn't conquered her shyness. "What were you wondering?" he asked.

"Well, I know you're a guide. Would you be willing to tell me something about Superstition Mountain? Davis and I are planning to hike in there and I'm not much of a camper."

Bram scowled and his annoyance showed in his voice. "The Superstitions are no place for amateur campers."

"I've already been told that. I was hoping you'd give me a few pointers."

Her persistence reminded him of another characteristic of Vala's—she was shy but stubborn. What the hell? He had time to spend an hour or so talking to her—it would take at least that long, he supposed, to convince her to try camping somewhere else. Besides, he was sort of curious to see what she looked like after fifteen years.

That didn't mean he was going to ask her into his home. Very few people even knew where he lived, much less got invited to visit. "You're in Apache Junction?" he said.

"Yes."

"There's a cafe in town called Auntie Mame's.

I'll meet you there in about forty-five minutes, okay?"

After hanging up, he didn't move for a minute or two. Vala Channing. At sixteen she'd been slender and fair-haired. Though not exactly pretty, there'd been something about her that caught his attention—maybe the somewhat exotic upward tilt to her blue eyes, eyes that reminded him of a spring sky, clear and unclouded. Or maybe the hesitant smile that lit her face on all-too-rare occasions.

It wasn't that he'd thought of her often over the years, because he hadn't. But, somehow, that one night they'd been together stuck in his memory with the tenacity of a cactus spine. And equally barbed.

In the booth at Auntie Mame's, Davis slurped the last of his chocolate shake through the straw and then eased back in his seat. "I still don't see why we can't just buy a tent and stuff and start off," he said. "We've got a map, haven't we?"

"Superstition Mountain isn't like the Catskills back home," Vala said. "I want Mr. Hunter's advice before we go any farther." What she'd actually hoped was that, once Bram recognized her name, he might offer to be their guide even though he'd taken his name off the list.

His gruffness on the phone had convinced her that would never come to pass. In fact, after his go-away-and-don't-bother-me manner, she was surprised he'd even agreed to meet her here—a meeting she was looking forward to with both anticipation and trepidation. She touched her hair with nervous fingers and ran her tongue over her lips. Did she have time to go the ladies' room to check her lipstick again? Probably not, but there ought to be a mirror somewhere in her shoulder bag. . . .

"Is that him?" Davis asked.

Vala stopped burrowing in her bag and glanced at the tall, dark-haired man striding toward their booth, suddenly finding she hardly had enough breath to say, "Yes," to Davis.

He stopped at the booth, his gaze holding hers for a long moment. "Vala," he said, nodding. Then he turned to look at her son. "I'm Bram Hunter," he said. "Do you mind if I sit next to you, Davis?"

"I guess not," Davis mumbled, sliding over to make room.

Bram eased onto the seat, said, "Coffee," to the approaching waitress and looked at Vala again. "Why the Superstitions?" he asked.

"It's a long story. Back in Westchester, where we live, Davis inherited a map from an old Apache."

"Ndee," Davis said almost inaudibly without looking at either of them.

Bram glanced at him. "Tell me about the man who gave you the map," he said to the boy.

"His name was Mokesh and he's dead." Davis ran the words together as though getting them out fast so he could withdraw into silence once again.

"He was Ndee?" Bram persisted.

Vala noted a glimmer of interest lighten her son's sullen face. "Mokesh said Apache was an enemy word."

"Do you know what Ndee means?" Bram asked.

Davis nodded. "The Dream People. I know lots about them. Like how their Thunder God makes Superstition Mountain his home. And about Swift Wind. And how the buffalo came to the Ndee."

Vala was amazed. Davis rarely spoke more than a word or two to strangers and then only if she insisted.

"Mokesh must have been a good friend of yours," Bram said.

"He was my best friend. And I was his. That's why he gave me the map when he knew it was his time to die."

"If you want to show it to me, I'd like to see the map."

"Sure. I got it right here in my pack." Davis unzipped the pack and removed the rolled deerskin wrapped in plastic.

The waitress set Bram's coffee in front of him and he pushed it across the table toward Vala, shoving the other dishes aside, too, to make room to spread out the deerskin map. His attention was fixed on Davis; not once did he look at Vala.

Both he and Davis bent over the map, Davis pointing to the various strange and primitive markings and telling Bram what Mokesh had said about them. "He told me when I came to the X, I'd find my heart's desire. So then I knew it was a treasure map."

"Heart's desire," Bram repeated. "Mokesh didn't say treasure?"

Davis shook his head. "But what else could he mean?"

They've both forgotten me, Vala thought. I might as well not be here in the booth. Despite being pleased that Davis had taken to Bram, it miffed her a little to be so totally ignored.

"Mom said I ought to make a paper copy of the map on account of the deerskin's so old and cracked and all," Davis said, "so I did." He pulled the copy from his pack and handed it to Bram.

After comparing the copy to the original, Bram nodded. "Good job."

"I tried to be careful." Davis's pleasure at the praise showed in his voice.

It occurred to Vala that she had never once, in the years before or after their divorce, heard Neal praise his son. Quite the opposite. Neal always seemed to be pointing up Davis's flaws. Two left feet. All thumbs. A snail could run faster. Couldn't throw a ball straight if your life depended on it. The name of the game is to *hit* the ball.

Neal blamed her. She couldn't count the times he'd said so, not caring whether Davis heard or not. Look at him—short and skinny, takes after your side of the family, even to the glasses, just like your old man.

It was true her father wore glasses. Unfortunately

for Davis, her bookish father was also disappointed in the boy because he wasn't much of a reader.

"So, are you going to help us find the treasure, Mr. Hunter?" Davis asked, startling Vala. "Are you going to be our guide?"

She hadn't thought to caution her son not to mention guiding because she hadn't dreamed Davis would come far enough out of his shell to say any more than he had to—certainly not to a stranger. She tensed, waiting for Bram's terse refusal—after all, he *had* crossed his name off the list.

Bram didn't reply immediately. Instead, he helped Davis roll up the deerskin. "I don't know if I can," he said at last, speaking to the boy rather than to Vala. "I've made plans that I'm not sure I can change."

He pulled a couple of bills from his pocket and jerked his head toward the electronic game at the back of the cafe. "Why don't you try your luck at zapping space monsters—my treat—while I discuss things with your mother?"

Davis hesitated but when Vala didn't say anything, he took the money Bram offered, saying, "Okay. Thanks."

Both she and Bram watched him until he got the bills changed, reached the machine and fed in the money. When the beeps and whizzes and other exotic noises began, Bram abruptly faced her.

"What in hell are you thinking of, letting your son believe in that map?" he demanded. "Or do *you* believe in it, too?"

Vala sat back and crossed her arms over her breasts. "I'm not saying the map will lead to treasure. But you must admit it *is* old. Like John Mokesh—he was in his nineties. And he was also an Apache. If anyone knew Superstition Mountain in the past, the Apache did."

Bram scowled. "I don't doubt this Mokesh was old but that doesn't mean the map is. Faking age with deerskin or paper isn't difficult. Do you have any idea how many different bogus maps of the Lost Dutchman Mine are in circulation? I've personally seen at least twenty variations and God only knows how many copies of each variation have been circulated since Jacob Walz died in 1891. Walz was the old Dutchman, in case you don't remember."

"I never heard of Jacob Walz. Or the Lost Dutchman Mine," she said indignantly. "What does that have to do with the map Mr. Mokesh gave my son?"

"Maps purporting to lead the way to treasure somewhere in the Superstitions are a dime a dozen. And not one of them worth a damn. Apparently people never ask themselves why, if the map leads to a gold mine, the person who sold it to them didn't use the map to find the gold himself. You're setting Davis up for a mighty big disappointment. Do you think that's fair?"

She glared at him. "You have no right to criticize what I'm doing. Especially when you haven't a clue as to the circumstances."

He glared right back at her. "What *are* the circumstances that would lead a mother to promise her son something she can't deliver?"

"I'm not promising Davis anything!" she cried, so furious at Bram's presumption that she forgot to be careful about what she said. "All I want is for him to be himself again. Except for John Mokesh, the map is the first thing my son has taken any real interest in for well over a year. He believes in that map. Do you expect me to tell him it's a fake and then watch him slump back into apathy? Well, I'm damn well not going to!"

"Keep your voice down," Bram warned, increasing her annoyance even though she knew he was right. She didn't care about the others in the cafe but Davis mustn't hear any of this.

Bram put his arms on the table and leaned toward her. "What *are* you going to do, then?"

"Follow the map into the Superstitions," she snapped. "That's what Davis wants and so that's what we'll do."

Bram shook his head. "I see you're still as stubborn as ever."

She unfolded her arms and pushed his cup of coffee toward him. "I'm not stubborn, just determined to help my son in any way I can."

He ignored the coffee. "But will this be a help in the long run?"

Vala didn't answer immediately. "I can't deal with long-range planning at the moment," she said finally. "I can only deal with today. I'm sorry to have bothered you—this is no concern of yours."

Belatedly realizing he probably was married, with children of his own, she added, "I guess I was so wound up in my own problems that I forgot everything else. I should have realized you'd have plans, this being a family time of year and all."

He half-smiled. "I'm one up on you—I didn't make the mistake of getting married. Apparently it was a mistake?"

Vala wasn't accustomed to sharing her private life with anyone, but since he already knew she was divorced, why not admit the truth? It wasn't as though she was confessing her innermost secrets to a total stranger.

"A mistake, yes. Maybe not the worst I've ever made but right up there near the top. But some good came of it—Davis."

"I like him." Surprise tinged Bram's words, whether because of the feeling or because he'd admitted to it. She wasn't sure.

She smiled, her anger at him gone. "So do I."

He smiled back and, for a moment, she felt something pass between them and go tingling along her nerves, making her feel more alive than she had in years. How could she have forgotten how dark his eyes were, or how he'd once made her feel when she'd gazed into them? She'd best remember that looking into Bram's eyes could prove to be a dangerous occupation.

"Strange, you showing up in town," he said.

"Not any stranger than me seeing your name on that guide list," she countered.

"Next time I'll have to remember to use a darker pen when I cross it out."

His words made the moment of awareness vanish as if it had never been.

Vala didn't realize the electronic noises had ceased until Davis appeared at the booth and Bram slid over to make room.

"How'd you do?" Bram asked.

Davis shrugged. "So-so." He glanced at Vala, then back at Bram. "Did you decide?" he asked.

"You have to answer a question of mine first," Bram said. "Have you ever ridden a horse?"

"Sure," Davis said. "I learned two years ago at camp and I go to the same place every summer so I get to practice."

Bram looked at Vala. "You?"

Since she'd figured he'd ask her next, she'd already made up her mind what she had to do. She nodded, avoiding Davis's eye.

"In that case," Bram said, "since I couldn't talk your mother out of the camping trip, it looks like it's up to me to keep you two greenhorns out of trouble."

"Yay!" Davis cried. "Can we start off right now?"

"Tomorrow morning early. You two have to get equipped first and I have to arrange for the horses and collect my own gear."

And cancel your plans, Vala thought, wondering

what Bram was giving up to be their guide. After his lecture to her about fake maps, she was amazed he'd changed his mind and agreed to take them. Her glow of happiness was, she assured herself, for Davis's sake.

Once he'd finished supervising her purchases at the camping store, Bram left them, saying he'd come by their motel at six the next morning so they could follow him to the place where the horses were.

"Be ready to roll," he warned.

"We will," Davis promised.

He was quiet on the ride back to the motel and so was she, going over and over in her mind that strange moment or two of silent communication between her and Bram. What did it mean? She took a deep breath and shook her head. Never mind what it meant, she had no intention of getting involved with any man. And certainly not Bram Hunter.

After they reached the motel and had carried their purchases into their room, Davis said, "I didn't want to say anything before in case Mr. Hunter might change his mind. But, Mom, you lied to him."

Vala nodded. "I know. I suppose I ought to be sorry. It was in a good cause, though."

"He'll find out real soon," Davis warned her.

"Maybe not. At least not right away. After all, what's so difficult about riding a horse?"

Davis rolled his eyes. "Whoa. I can't believe you

said that. You don't even know how to get on a horse."

"So you'll teach me how before tomorrow. I'm a quick study."

"I can tell you how to mount a horse," he said, "but there's a lot more to it than that. Mom, you're gonna be really, really sorry."

TWO

The wariness in the kid's eyes had decided him, Bram thought as he tucked his denim shirt into his jeans in the early morning darkness. Though Davis, fair-haired and blue-eyed, didn't look anything like the young boy Bram had once been, he'd recognized a kindred spirit, a lonely, confused youngster on his way to becoming embittered.

Bram knew the feeling well and he meant to do his damnedest to make an adventure out of this trip into the Superstitions. Since talking with Vala and her son had convinced him that Davis was determined to believe in the fake deerskin map, he'd try to give the boy some excitement to make up for the disappointment that was bound to come when Davis discovered the old Apache's gift didn't point the way to a treasure lode.

Ndee, not Apache—Davis was right. Not that it made a hell of a lot of difference.

In any case, Bram wasn't giving up his long-planned trip to the Caribbean for Vala's sake. Not at all. It was for her son. No nine-year-old boy should have to feel rejected. *Rejected.* Bram gritted his teeth, reminded of what he'd long ago buried with the rest of his unhappy past.

Vala obviously loved her son, but what she'd told him, combined with what he'd seen in Davis's eyes, had echoed in Bram's heart. He knew from his own experience that the love of a mother never quite made up for an absent, uncaring father.

If I was worth anything, he'd pay attention to me. Did those words haunt Davis as they had young Bram?

I can't solve the problem, Bram told himself, but I can do my best to give Davis a slam-bang western adventure to take home with him.

As for Vala—well, what about her? He'd be lying if he didn't admit she still appealed to him. Or that what had happened years ago didn't still rankle. Gentlemen never stooped to getting even, he reminded himself—but then no one had ever accused him of being a gentleman. He half-smiled, contemplating the enforced togetherness of a camping trip with pleasurable anticipation.

All right, so he had more than one motive for agreeing to take mother and son into the mountains. So what? Both he and Vala were over thirty—God, where had the years gone?—and free of entanglements.

He finished pulling on his boots and strode to the kitchen to get his wake-me-up slug of coffee before driving the pickup to the Apache Junction motel to pick up his two happy campers. He'd already told them they'd have breakfast at the horse ranch.

His evaluation of Vala went up a notch when he found both her and her son ready to go. He had little patience with dawdlers. "Pancakes and sausage at Brenden's Bronco Corral," he told Davis.

Davis glanced at his mother before saying, "There's a whole lot of cholesterol in sausages."

"We'll work it off, I promise you," Bram assured him. "And while we're on the subject of food—" He paused to look at Vala before turning back to Davis. "Everybody eats what the cook—that's me—packs in. The first complainer gets to take over the cooking."

Vala lifted her hands. "Hey, I'm on vacation. You won't hear any complaints from me."

"Me neither," Davis agreed, eyeing the pickup wistfully. "I found out in summer camp that cooking over a campfire is hard."

"Want to ride with me?" Bram asked him.

"Okay, Mom?"

Vala nodded and Davis wasted no time climbing into the cab of the truck.

"You'll be following me on up the Apache Trail—that's Route 88—for about four miles," Bram told Vala. "You'll see a sign for Brenden's to the right. We'll turn off there."

She nodded and got into her small rental car, packed with camping gear. As she pulled onto the highway after his truck, she tried not to think about what was to come after the pancakes and sausages at Brenden's. As the time crept closer to actually mounting a horse, she became more and more nervous.

Before they went to bed last night, she'd picked Davis's brain for all the tips he could remember about riding and horses and discovered there was more to it than she'd imagined. You even had to get on the animal from a certain side.

"You mean to tell me the horse will know the difference if I try to mount him from his right side instead of his left?" she'd asked. "Who made up these rules anyway?"

"They told us at summer camp that in the olden days the knights used to carry their swords on their left side so it was easier for them to throw their right leg over the saddle first. I guess it just sort of became a tradition to train horses that way."

"I'm never going to remember all this stuff," she muttered.

"Don't sweat it, Mom," he'd advised finally. "Just remember that you and not the horse are in charge and you'll be okay."

I shouldn't have any trouble with that, she thought now. I'm a human and humans are smarter than horses.

All she had to do was get into the saddle without mishap and then her horse would follow the one ahead of him. Or so Davis had assured her. She ought to be able to manage that. In fact, she had to or she'd give herself away and Bram might well back out of the trip altogether. For Davis's sake, that mustn't happen.

All of this was for Davis's sake. It really didn't make any difference that the idea of following the old map into the mountains had much more appeal to her ever since Bram had offered to guide them. Why shouldn't it? He was not only a camping expert but also someone she'd known in the past. Not a friend, exactly, but not a stranger either.

Who knew? Maybe they'd *be* friends by the time the trip was over. She found herself humming "Getting To Know You" and stopped abruptly. Getting to know Bram was not the reason she was on this journey.

Though the sun wasn't up, to her right she could see the dark silhouette of Superstition Mountain against the lightening sky. On the flat land to the left, a lone saguaro cactus thrust up two giant arms as though welcoming her back to the country where she'd been born.

Vala knew that Phoenix was a green oasis in the midst of dry country, but she hadn't clearly remembered how desert-like the surroundings actually were. Not sand dune desert but arid country where little grew except cacti and small trees like the palo verde that could make do without much water. She'd grown accustomed to the greenery of the east coast, but somehow this starkness seemed right to her, giving her a strange feeling she'd come home.

Could this feeling have anything to do with seeing Bram Hunter again?

Vala shook her head in denial. She'd already made one mistake in choosing a man; she had no intention of making another. Not that Bram had given her any reason to believe he wanted to be chosen! In fact, she'd gotten the impression he didn't think much of her.

He'd made it very clear that in his opinion the map was a fake and he'd blamed her for encouraging her son to believe in a treasure. She was well aware Bram was guiding them only because he'd taken a liking to Davis and had come to the conclusion that nothing he said would prevent her from bringing her son into the Superstitions with or without a guide.

I wouldn't want it any other way, she told herself firmly. Since Bram's not interested in me, I can relax and not worry about being more or less alone with him for the next week.

In any case, the presence of a nine-year-old was a powerful deterrent to romance, even if this particular one, once he fell asleep, couldn't easily be roused by anything less than a twenty-one-gun salute. Besides, she didn't *want* a romance.

The sun was up by the time they reached Brenden's Bronco Corral—something out of a western movie. Davis was entranced, looking around excitedly as Mac Brenden greeted Bram with the ease of long acquaintance, then sized up her and Davis. Davis seemed to pass muster but she thought Mac's shrewd blue eyes saw through her brave assertion that "any horse will do."

Tense with foreboding, she could only make a pretense of enjoying the excellent pancakes and sizzling sausage. All too soon, the time came for her to actually get into—or was it onto?—the saddle of her mount.

"Susie Q's a real easygoer," Mac assured her. "Getting on a bit but that makes for a smart trail horse. You can't go wrong with old Susie."

Her son and Bram were already mounted, Bram on a frisky chestnut gelding named Fremont and Davis on a much smaller gelding that Mac had called a Morgan. "Wish I had a dozen as dependable as Nate," he'd said. "You can't beat a Morgan for stamina combined with an even disposition."

Taking a deep breath and reciting under her breath what her son had told her, Vala approached the mare. From the left. Standing even with the saddle, facing Susie Q, she took the reins into her left hand, then placed that hand firmly on the mare's neck and her right on the saddle horn. Relieved that Susie Q didn't move, she managed to get her left foot into the stirrup and tried her best to brace her knee against the horse. Now came the tricky part.

Pushing with her right foot, she sprang up until she was standing in the stirrup. At this point she almost lost her balance but leaned forward in time to avoid a fall. She swung her right leg over the saddle and there she was, sitting square in the saddle, on top of Susie Q.

Flushed with triumph, she glanced around only

to discover nobody was watching her. They'd all, even Davis, taken it for granted she could mount a horse. This is only the beginning, she reminded herself. Keep your mind on what to do next—heels down, hold the reins neither loose nor tight with your index finger between the two strips of leather. Don't ever hang on to the saddle horn.

In addition to the three riding horses, Bram had arranged for a packhorse. Loaded with their gear, the packhorse followed Bram's Fremont, then came Nate with Davis. She and Susie Q brought up the rear.

Good, she thought. If I make mistakes Bram won't be so likely to notice them.

Davis had told her to lean slightly forward and move with the horse, but she soon discovered that was easier said than done. Still, she wasn't too uncomfortable until they passed through the gates of the horse ranch and Bram increased Fremont's pace from a walk to what she thought might be a trot. Obediently, the other horses matched the leader's gait.

No matter what she tried to do, she kept bouncing up and down in the saddle rather than moving with Susie Q. Though jarring, it didn't bother her too much. At first.

The morning was cool enough to be coat weather, in her case a lined denim jacket. In addition she wore a broad-brimmed hat, jeans and a pair of riding boots comfortable enough to hike in, boots that Bram had suggested she buy. Davis wore a similar outfit. Bram, she'd noticed, looked like a real, honest-to-goodness cowboy.

The horses followed a trail toward Superstition Mountain, passing between clumps of ocotillo and various large round cacti that were all leaning toward the southwest. Beyond the vegetation close to the trail were various other unfriendly-looking plants whose wicked spines and spikes made her want to grab hold of the saddle horn just in case Susie Q took a notion to buck and send her flying head over teakettle. She resisted the temptation, reminding herself that the mare was not only a tried-and-true trail horse but seemed to have a placid disposition as well.

The Superstitions loomed ahead, far more rugged looking at close range than from the highway. Near the topmost peaks, the sun glinted off a broad white streak running across the otherwise reddish brown rocks making up the mountain. Unlike New York's Catskills, Superstition Mountain had no foothills; it rose straight up. Daunted and awed by the forbidding crags facing her, she realized how foolish she'd been to think of tackling this mountain without a guide.

By the time the horses entered the mountains via a cobble-strewn wash and began to pick their way up a steep ridge, Vala's muscles were aching. Surely Bram would halt soon for a rest, she told herself. As the trail grew steeper, she realized that, even if they did stop, she wouldn't have enough room to dismount and ease her aches and pains. There was no choice but to grin and bear it.

The rocky, tumbled terrain around them seemed as confusing as a maze. The only consistent feature was a vast stone pillar rising in the distance— Weaver's Needle. In addition to the stands of prickly pear cactus and the grayish jojoba shrubs, green-barked palo verde trees were strewn at random among the rocks, making her wonder how they found enough dirt to grow.

After a while she stopped noticing what was around her because she hurt too much to pay attention to anything but her own discomfort. When Susie Q finally quit moving, it took Vala a moment or two to realize they'd stopped on a small plateau. Bram and Davis had already dismounted and both were looking expectantly at her. Unfortunately, though she remembered Davis had told her to get off a horse the same way she got on, only in reverse, she was in too much pain to be able to recall how she'd mounted. And even if she did remember, she wasn't sure her aching muscles would obey her.

Bram ambled toward her. "Thought we'd take a rest here," he said, obviously waiting for her to dismount.

I can simply fall off, she told herself, or I can admit to the truth. Taking a deep breath, which hurt, she let it out slowly and admitted the truth. "I can't get off unless you help me."

His eyebrows rose and he shook his head. "Stubborn," he muttered. "Have you *ever* been on a horse before?"

"No. And it won't do any good for you to tell me how to dismount because I hurt too much to try."

He scowled at her. "If you got on, you can get off. Listen up. Keep hold of the reins while you put your left hand on Susie Q's neck. Now put your right hand on the saddle horn. Good. Lean slightly forward and shift your weight to the left stirrup."

Vala groaned as she obeyed. When he told her to swing her right leg over the saddle, it took her two tries and a few more groans before she managed it. She was certain she'd never be able to step straight down and free her left foot from the stirrup as she did so, and she was right. If Bram hadn't caught her, extricating her from the stirrup at the same time, she would have sprawled onto the ground with her left foot still caught in the damn stirrup.

She clung to Bram, hurting all over, not sure she could stand by herself, in too much pain to feel humiliated. Susie Q snorted and, when Vala involuntarily glanced at her, she found the mare had turned her head and was staring, quite possibly in disgust, at this tenderfoot rider who couldn't even dismount properly.

With Bram's help, she hobbled a few steps but, when she tried to ease down so she could stretch out on the ground, he wouldn't let her, saying, "You won't be able to get up if you do."

"I don't care," she mumbled.

"I do." His voice was hard and cold. "We're not going to camp early just for your convenience. You lied to me and you're going to suffer the consequences. We'll rest for a bit; then either we go on or we turn around and give up any idea of camping in the Superstitions."

Vala wanted nothing more than to get back to the motel as fast as possible and fall onto the bed, but one look at Davis's face made her give up the idea. She didn't know how she'd manage it, but she would go on. Even if it killed her.

"You may have to lift me onto the horse," she told Bram, "but I'm not giving up."

"Way to go, Mom," Davis said.

"You may think so," Bram growled, "but by the time we camp this afternoon, your mother is going to be extremely sorry she didn't choose the other alternative."

"I think she was afraid you wouldn't guide us if she told you she couldn't ride," Davis said.

She was right, Bram thought. He wouldn't have. His annoyance with her was mixed with reluctant admiration for her tenacity. Vala just wasn't the kind who gave up, even when the odds were against her.

"We'll walk the horses for the next stretch and give them a rest," he said, aware he was doing it for Vala's sake. The horses weren't anywhere near ridden out but neither she nor Davis would know that. While she'd find walking painful, it wouldn't hurt as much as getting back into the saddle.

They went on, Vala hobbling gamely along, leading Susie Q. Bram decided that Mac must have had a sixth sense about Vala's nonexistent riding skills, because the mare was the most amiable and tractable horse in his corral. Susie Q would never take advantage of her rider.

Near noon he called a halt for lunch and they ate the cheese sandwiches put up for them at Brenden's, Vala leaning against a rocky outcropping rather than trying to sit. When they were ready to go on, he hoisted her into the saddle, watching her bite her lip rather than moan as her aching muscles protested.

When they finally reached the spot where, revising his original plans, he'd decided to camp for the night, it was only three in the afternoon but he knew she couldn't go on much longer. He'd originally figured three days in and three days out, but now he added two additional days to his estimate. Food wouldn't be a problem because he always brought more than he expected to need.

After Davis helped Bram with the horses, they put up the tent where the boy and his mother would sleep. "It sure goes faster with four hands than it does with two," Bram told him when they finished. "Thanks."

Davis nodded, flushing with pleasure, then turned to look at Vala who was sprawled on a sleeping bag, eyes closed. "Do you think she'll feel better tomorrow?"

"Some, anyway."

"Where's your tent?" Davis asked.

"I like looking up at the stars so I don't use a tent unless it rains."

"I've slept outside before," Davis said. "At camp. I don't need to be in the tent with my mom."

"For her sake you should be, tonight at least," Bram told him. "She might need you."

"Yeah, you're right."

Vala heard them talking but, in her relief at being able to stretch out at last, she didn't bother to pay attention to what they said until Davis knelt beside her, insisting she take a pill, claiming that Bram said it would help her.

"Mr. Hunter," she mumbled reflexively.

"He says on the trail we use first names."

She opened her eyes and Davis showed her the pill. "Ibu-something," he said. "It's for sore muscles."

"Ibuprofen." She raised herself onto one elbow, swallowed the pill with a sip of water, then fell back onto the sleeping bag and didn't move again until sunset, when it was time to eat Bram's camp stew served with biscuits and hot tea.

She managed to walk to the campfire by herself, where she sat on a folded sleeping bag, her back propped against a second rolled-up bag while she ate.

"Tonight's lesson," Bram announced, "is what to do if you get lost."

"You serve lessons with the meals?" she asked.

"Our walking wounded must be mending," Bram said to Davis. "She's beginning to talk." Turning to her, he added, "One lesson each evening—you might call it dessert."

"A kid at my camp got lost on a hike once," Davis said. "He wandered around until he came to a road and some guy on one of those big Harleys gave him a ride back to camp."

"We don't have any bikers in the Superstitions," Bram said, "so listen up. Rule one. As soon as you know you're lost, stop, sit down and try to figure out where you are in relation to where you came from. Use your head, not your legs. Rule two. If you have no idea where you are, make camp in a nearby sheltered spot. Rule three. Don't wander. If you must move, travel downhill. Rule four. If you're hurt, try to light a fire and make a smoke signal. Rule five. Don't yell, run or get panicky. And never give up."

Vala closed her eyes and let his words flow over her, thinking that when he wasn't angrily growling, Bram's deep voice was really quite soothing.

When Bram finished, he and Davis cleaned up, leaving her sitting alone by the fire. If she didn't try to move, she was fairly comfortable. But then Davis returned, asking for his sleeping bag, the one she was leaning against.

"I'm going to turn in, Mom," he said. "We've

been climbing all day and the higher elevation makes you tired, you know."

She didn't argue, aware that, though he might be using it as an excuse for feeling sleepy so early in the evening, he actually was telling the truth. He took his sleeping bag to the tent, leaving her still sitting but now uncomfortably. She was trying to gather the energy as well as the courage—it was going to hurt—to clamber to her feet when Bram came back to the fire carrying her unrolled sleeping bag and the old gray sweat suit she'd tucked inside it.

"You planning to sleep in these?" he asked.

Taken aback, she stammered, "Uh—yes."

He dropped the clothes on her lap. "Get into them."

Before she could think what to do or say, he walked off, making it clear he didn't plan to stay and watch.

She shrugged, wincing at the soreness in her shoulders, and thought, Why not? I have to get undressed sooner or later and it'll be easier here than in the tent.

When Bram returned, she was standing with the sweats on and trying to decide if she could manage to bend over and retrieve the clothes she'd discarded. He knelt and rolled her clothes into a bundle, then smoothed her sleeping bag. "Lie on this," he ordered.

She stared at him in confusion.

He half-smiled and pulled a tube from his jacket

pocket. "Liniment. Good for sore muscles. Don't forget you have to get back on Susie Q tomorrow."

Vala grimaced at the thought.

"This liniment won't cure you," he added, "but you have my personal guarantee it'll help."

Deciding she couldn't feel any worse, Vala eased herself down onto the sleeping bag, lying on her stomach. She tensed when he lifted her sweatshirt and put his hand on her bare back.

"Relax," he ordered.

She tried to obey. His hands were warm, the liniment cool at first, then, as he rubbed it in, pleasantly hot. He kneaded her muscles with an incredibly gentle touch.

"That feels good," she murmured, thinking, as he went on to her lower back, that perhaps it felt a little too good for her peace of mind.

Good wasn't exactly the word he'd choose, Bram thought as his hands stroked the curve of her hip. When he decided the liniment might help her, it hadn't occurred to him just what the treatment was going to do to him.

Her skin was so soft and smooth, satiny under his fingers, and when he cupped her rounded buttocks he found himself imagining her in his arms, tight against him while he held her like this. . . .

Keep your mind on what you're doing, Hunter, he warned himself as desire began to throb insistently through him. You're supposed to be a masseur at the moment, not a lover.

Why was touching Vala different from touching

any other woman? Because she'd been a mystery he'd never had a chance to solve?

He'd thought he came on this trip for the kid's sake, but he had to admit that sure as hell wasn't the way it looked now.

THREE

Vala slept so soundly she didn't hear Davis get up, dress and leave the tent. She roused to a loud clanging, sitting up abruptly, then wincing as her sore muscles protested the sudden move.

"Breakfast, Mom!" Davis shouted from somewhere outside the tent. She wondered if he was the one who'd banged on a pan with a spoon or if that was Bram's idea of fun.

"I'm awake," she called back.

She dressed as quickly as she could, ignoring the twinges, trying to convince herself riding would prove easier today, and joined the two males. The morning air held a touch of crispness that she knew the sun would soon banish.

"Bram's oatmeal is way cool," Davis informed her. "He puts cinnamon in it."

Vala raised her eyebrows. Davis eating oatmeal? The stuff he called gooey yuck when she tried to serve it at home?

"Sticks to the ribs, with or without cinnamon," Bram said. "Good on the trail. Right, partner?"

Davis nodded with enthusiasm.

Once finished with breakfast, Bram said, "Today's dessert is a message from the chain fruit cholla." He pointed at a gangly-looking cactus to their left. "The cholla warns, 'Brush against me and I'll break off a chunk of myself to attach to you. Trust me, you won't like it.' "

"Isn't that what we used to call jumping cactus?" Vala asked.

He nodded.

"Did you guys really go to high school together like Mom said?" Davis asked. "I mean when you were teenagers." He sounded dubious about the possibility of either of them ever having been that young.

Bram grinned at him. "Yup. In fact, I can even remember way, way back when I was nine, like you are now. I was a really rotten kid. But I grew up and learned how to behave—when I work at it. Speaking of work, time to pack up and hit the trail."

Vala and Davis pitched in to help, although her painful muscles slowed her considerably. All too soon it was time to climb aboard Susie Q once more, whether she wanted to or not. Bram had already saddled the mare—she supposed that would be the next thing she'd have to learn—so all she had to do right now was remember how to get on.

The first thing she forgot was which was the mounting side and she approached from the wrong one, earning an astounded look from Susie Q.

"Mom!" Davis yelled. "Get on her other side!"

As Vala switched, she thanked her lucky stars for the mare's patience and placidity. If she had to ride, at least she had an unflappable horse that forgave her mistakes. She got up onto Susie Q with no difficulty despite her aches, but as soon as they started off single file, she groaned. How she was going to endure one more day of this, much less four or more, heaven only knew.

Up ahead of her she heard Davis whistling, something he hadn't done in months, and she resigned herself. If he was happy, what were a few aches and pains?

"All right back there in the rear?" Bram called.

"Yo!" Davis answered.

A lot of the problem was in *her* rear, Vala thought ruefully, her affirmation a lot less enthusiastic than her son's.

But as they rode on, she felt herself loosening up and settling into Susie Q's rhythm without consciously willing it. As she'd predicted, the rising sun's heat began to warm the crisp air and little chirping birds—cactus wrens, maybe?—flitted back and forth. Vala had always enjoyed the outdoors. She couldn't deny the day was beautiful and her companions cheerful company, Bram, now whistling in counterpoint to Davis.

Bram was so good with her son. She could wish he'd donate a few dabs of his considerateness to her, but she didn't expect it. Although, come to think of it, massaging her sore muscles with that liniment last night was thoughtful. She didn't think he'd realized how his hands on her body had done more than ease muscle aches. If he had, she'd rather not be aware of it.

There'd always been something about Bram that had turned her on—not that she ever planned to let him know it. He was every bit as good-looking as he'd been as a teenager, with the added attraction maturity brings. Easy does it, she warned herself.

When they stopped to rest the horses, she was pleasantly surprised to find she was able to dismount without help and without falling on her face.

Looked like they'd be going on, Bram thought, watching Vala covertly. She was smiling today, even though he could tell by the way she moved that she still hurt. Definitely not the droopy, sorry-for-herself type he couldn't bear, but then she never had been. Kind of a loner in high school, as he remembered. Though she'd had friends, she hadn't been a part of any of the in crowds.

"I might just turn into a real horsewoman and surprise everyone." Vala was speaking to her son but he knew she wanted him to hear.

"Might," he said. "Might not."

"You don't faze me," she told him. "Susie Q's as smart as they come. You'd be amazed at what she's taught me already."

"I'm not a bad teacher myself—depending on what you want to learn," he said with a grin.

He could see she wasn't sure she wanted to reply to that one. Davis saved her the trouble of deciding by saying, "Yeah, Mom, he knows a lot of neat stuff."

"I'll bet," she muttered.

"How much?" Bram asked her.

"How much what?"

"Do you want to bet?"

"I'm not entirely sure what we're supposed to be betting on."

"My mom doesn't ever bet money," Davis put in.

Bram raised an eyebrow.

"He's talking about the state lotteries," she said. "I don't do them."

"I wasn't thinking about money," Bram told her.

She shot him what was meant to be a quelling glance, but he had no intention of dropping this. "What I meant was," he drawled, "I'm willing to bet I can teach you to do something you never dreamed you could do."

"Like bungee jumping? No, thanks."

"We'll exclude death-defying stunts. Scared to take me up on it?"

Again Davis took her off the hook by saying, "Whoa, look at that weird lizard." He pointed.

Just before it slithered into a crevice, Bram saw the big, brownish lizard whose skin appeared too big for him.

"That's a chuckwalla," he said. "Nonpoisonous. They like these mountains."

"There's a lizard drawn on my map," Davis said. "It's the first marker.

Bram nodded. "I think I know what it refers to. We ought to get there sometime this afternoon." He eyed Vala appraisingly.

Following his gaze, Davis said, "Aw, Mom's doing better. She can make it."

After that, Vala felt she had no choice, even though she grew less and less comfortable on Susie Q's back as the day wore on. She was almost past the point of caring when Bram finally called a halt.

"This'll be our night camp," he said. "After we take care of the horses, we'll hike a bit and I'll show you the marker."

Hike? When it was all she could do to get herself off the horse? How she longed to stretch out on the ground and not move for hours. Maybe days. Gritting her teeth, she controlled the impulse, aware once down she wouldn't willingly get up.

The marker turned out to be a rock formation off the trail that to her only vaguely looked like a lizard. Davis, though, was thrilled at the validation of his map and chattered on about finding treasure all the while he helped set up camp.

Vala, by then lying fully dressed on her sleeping bag in a half-doze, was barely aware of what he was saying, though she did hear Bram.

"Treasure comes in different packages," he said. "Sometimes you don't recognize it right away as treasure."

"But this treasure's gold," Davis protested. "Everyone knows what that looks like."

"Old Mokesh didn't tell you it was gold. He didn't even say treasure."

"Uh, no, he didn't. But he must've known what it was 'cause he had the map. I figured it has to be gold on account of Lost Dutchman Mine and all, you know? But maybe it's jewels and stuff—is that what you mean?"

"No, not jewels. We'll talk more about it later. Right now you'd better get your mother up or she'll miss supper. When I cook, no one skips meals."

Vala groaned at the ultimatum, but realized she was too hungry to bypass supper. Getting stiffly to her feet, she joined them at the small campfire.

After they'd eaten, Vala made no pretense of helping to clean up because she was just too sore. As the fire died down to coals, Bram and Davis came to sit by her.

"We might run into some weather tomorrow," Bram said.

Vala gazed up at the dark sky. The moon hadn't risen but she could see stars. "How can you tell?" she asked.

"Mom, he's a guide. He knows the area."

Bram chuckled. "I can't take the credit, partner. What I do is make sure I watch the Weather Channel to catch the five-day forecast before I go into the Superstitions."

"Hey, cool," Davis said.

Apparently nothing could tarnish her son's image of Bram as a western expert, full of all kinds of esoteric lore, even if it came from the TV, Vala thought a bit sourly. Then she wondered if maybe she was overreacting. Could she be the least bit jealous of Davis's hero worship?

Shame on her if she was. Her son needed a man's company, needed the kind of positive attention Bram was giving him. Thank heaven she didn't need such a thing. At least not from Bram.

"The thing is, lightning is always dangerous in the mountains," Bram said. "Rain's a nuisance, but neither people nor horses melt so we could keep going wet, if we had to. Lightning's another matter. We're not up near any of the peaks yet—they're the most dangerous in a storm—but tomorrow we may need to take shelter in a safer place than the trail."

"Mokesh told me the Old Ones sometimes try to keep people away from the Superstitions," Davis said. "Maybe they know we have that map and so they're sending the storm to try to drive us out."

"A storm is a natural force," Vala protested.

"Yeah, I know, but the Old Ones use nature, Mokesh said."

Vala stuck to her guns. "Whoever the Old Ones were, I doubt the coming storm has anything to do with them."

Davis was unconvinced. "You said were, but it's

are. Mokesh told me the Old Ones are still here, guarding the mountains."

Bram shifted uneasily. *Old Ones*. His grandmother had spoken of them. Not people, spirits. If you believe as the Ndee did. He shook his head. That part of him was long gone.

"You have to remember that Mokesh's world was not ours," Vala told her son. "Is not ours," she corrected.

"Okay, but we're *in* his world now. Maybe we don't know everything about it."

"Suppose we leave it at that for the moment," Bram said firmly, not wanting to be drawn into an argument that involved the Ndee. Ever. "What we need to do tomorrow is keep an eye out for the next marker the map shows. If it's a rock formation like the lizard was, we might be able to spot it in the distance."

"A bear, Mom," Davis said. "Remember to look for something like a bear."

"Not a real one, I hope!"

"No danger of that, not here," Bram told her.

"Good. Lizards don't faze me, not even gila monsters as long as they don't get too close. But I don't care to come up against an animal that's a lot bigger than I am."

"Wish we'd see a gila monster," Davis said wistfully. "It'd be cool to have a lizard for a pet."

"No reptiles." Vala's voice was so definite that Bram figured they'd had this argument before.

"Well, gee, we can't have a dog 'cause of the condo rules and I don't want fish."

"How about cats?" Bram asked, remembering Sheba's batch of kittens. His friend Nick was looking after them all and he hoped they were doing well.

"Mom?" Davis asked.

"There's nothing in the rules preventing cats," she said.

"Great," Bram said. "I just happen to have a few Siamese kittens that'll be looking for new homes soon. How do you feel about cats, Davis?"

"I never had one on account of my dad was allergic. But I'm not. Would you really give me a kitten?"

"You can take your pick once the Old Ones allow us to leave the mountains."

"Aw—you're like Mom. You don't really believe in them. I wish you could've talked to Mokesh. I really miss him." Davis yawned widely.

"Time to hit the old sleeping bag, partner," Bram said. "Dawn comes early."

After Davis somewhat reluctantly retired to the tent, Bram said to Vala, "Muscles still sore?"

She nodded. "Not quite so bad, though."

"Told you that liniment works. It's in my gear—I'll get it while you change and give you another rubdown." Without waiting for her to agree or disagree, he left the dying fire.

He took his time and, when he returned, she was in the gray sweats she used for camp sleeping. "I'm not so sure this is a good idea," she said.

"Harmless, wouldn't hurt a child," he said, well aware she wasn't referring to the liniment. He also agreed that maybe it wasn't such a good idea, considering how aroused he'd gotten the night before. But, he told himself, he'd risk it because she needed the rubdown so she'd feel better tomorrow.

As soon as his hands touched her bare skin, he realized he'd been lying to himself. He'd wanted to touch her, wanted the feel of her skin, soft and smooth under his fingers, wanted to run his hands over the sweet curve of her butt, to linger along her sides where he could feel the swell of her breasts. In fact, he wanted a hell of a lot more from Vala.

Not that he was likely to get it, even if he was unwise enough to try.

Vala's increased awareness of Bram made his massage far more erotic for her than it had been before. She tried in vain to block out those feelings and concentrate on the easing of her aching muscles. Instead, she found herself wanting him to go on and on, to touch her in places that had begun to ache for a far different reason than riding a horse.

Catching herself just before a moan of pure pleasure escaped, she said, "Enough!"

"You're right." His voice held the same husky catch she'd heard in her own. "Or maybe wrong," he added as he stopped and moved away from her. "Maybe it's not nearly enough."

His words jolted Vala. What did he mean? If she agreed it wasn't enough, what might happen? Unable to decide what to say or to face the matter head-on, the only thing she could think of to do was ignore what he'd said.

"I could use another ibuprofen, if you have one," she told him.

Once in the tent with her sound-asleep son, Vala didn't dissolve into sleep as easily as she had the night before. It was as though she could still feel Bram's hands on her body, stroking, arousing. . . .

It made her remember how she daydreamed about him when she was in high school. Not that she'd thought about him caressing her—a kiss was as far as she'd taken her fantasy. She'd longed to have him notice her, to think she was beautiful— even if she didn't believe she was—and to ask her for a date.

Not that she would have been allowed to go out with him if he had asked. Not only was he older, but he was also, in the eyes of parents of daughters at least, dangerous. But that wasn't the only reason she found him fascinating. She carried around like a treasure the one time their glances had crossed when they passed in the hall.

His eyes, dark and fathomless, promised a delicious wickedness she couldn't quite imagine, though she was willing enough to experience it. His hair, equally dark, long and lustrous, never stringy, framed a high-cheekboned face, a different face, one that made her tingle inside every time she saw him.

So here she was in the Superstitions with the guy. And he still intrigued her, she may as well admit it. Turned her on as well, since she was being honest with herself.

She definitely was not going to act on the attraction, though. Never. After all, there was Davis to consider. Davis, who could and did sleep though vast amounts of noise and commotion. . . .

Stop it, she warned herself. You are not going to throw yourself at Bram or even hint you might be available. You're going to behave in a mature fashion, which doesn't even include the possibility of involvement. He probably isn't really interested in you anyway.

Lying awake, looking up at the stars, Bram saw the first tiny cloud drift across them. Weather coming, definitely. Whatever the storm proved to be like, though, it'd be nothing compared to his own inner storm warnings.

Vala had been the one he'd always noticed in high school. He hadn't been sure why. For one thing, she'd had a long neck that made her look graceful. For another, her aloofness made her mysterious—what was she really like? Pretty enough in a different, less obvious way than some of the

other good-looking girls. Fragile was the word that
had come to him then.

In reality, Vala had turned out to be anything but
fragile. She'd married the wrong man, obviously,
but had the courage to divorce him and raise her
son alone. She'd even been prepared to venture into
these dangerous mountains alone to try to make
Davis happy, foolish as that expedition would have
been.

And so here they were, and he wanted her with
a much fiercer need than the boy he'd been in high
school. Then he hadn't taken his desire any farther
than maybe imagining kissing her because, for
some reason, he couldn't picture himself doing
anything more. Not with Vala Channing, even given
that she'd allow it, which he'd doubted.

What would be her reaction now? She'd certainly
given him no reason to think she'd been attracted
to him when they were teenagers. Did she feel any
differently now? Was he the only one feeling the
intangible link between them? He didn't think so.
He could sense she was as aware of him as he was
of her.

Best to leave it alone—he knew that. Always a
mistake to get involved with a woman you were
paid to guide. Business and pleasure needed to be
kept apart. Making love with Vala would be a risk.
Unfortunately, he was a risk taker. Not so daring
a one as he'd been as a teenager, but risk was an
intrinsic part of him, impossible to eradicate.

From somewhere far off a coyote howled at the

moon. The Ndee thought of Old Man Coyote as a trickster. If he believed in the Old Ones he might think he was being warned. Or challenged.

Remembering the feel of Vala's body under his hands, he smiled, anticipating the challenge to come.

FOUR

The next morning the sky was overcast when they saddled up. Feeling much more like herself, Vala made sure to watch just how Susie Q's saddle went on. Maybe tomorrow she'd try doing it.

After about an hour on the trail, they all heard a faint rumble of far-off thunder. Minutes later, Bram pulled off the trail, guiding them to a small flat-topped rise that rose several feet above the rest of the niche in the rock wall. Two rugged-looking crags loomed above them.

"Let's get the tent up," he said.

With Vala lending a hand, they soon had her tent ready, plus an extension fastened on and the gear stored inside. As the first raindrops fell, Bram rechecked the horses' tethers and then eased into the tent with her and Davis.

"How come you picked this place?" Davis asked.

"We're not in a hurry, so why not stay dry instead of wet?" he said. "Best to get off the trail anyway. If this turns into a gully washer, water comes pouring down the rocks like a river. Doesn't do to get swept away."

Lightning flashed and a close crack of thunder startled Vala.

"Just like Mokesh said." Davis spoke excitedly. "The thunder spirit really does live here."

Vala had never been afraid of thunderstorms, but she felt a lot more vulnerable in this tent than she'd ever been in a house.

"Close!" she cried as a brilliant shaft of lightning heralded a reverberating boom. Rain thrummed on the tent.

Close also applied to their quarters. The extension held most of the gear, including saddles, leaving the three of them crowded into the main tent, which was really intended for sleeping. At the moment, the sleeping bags were unrolled on top of the ground cloth for them to sit on.

"You know what Mokesh would say?" Davis asked. Without waiting for an answer he went on. "Bad weather's the time to tell stories 'cause the snakes aren't out so they can't hear."

"What have the snakes got to do with it?" Vala asked.

"If the weather's good they might be hiding close by and hear," Bram said. "There are some stories the snakes don't want people to tell."

She looked at him, astonished.

Davis took the information in stride. "Yeah, you got that right, according to what Mokesh said. So who's gonna go first?"

"How about you, partner?" Bram said, pleasing Vala, who could see Davis was bursting to tell one.

"It's a story I heard from Mokesh," Davis began. "Some things about it I don't understand real well, but it's a story about how an old Ndee medicine man named Wandering Shadow found the pouch lost by the Great Spirit."

He went on to tell about Wandering Shadow getting lost in a blizzard and discovering a shining warrior lying in the snow. "He built a fire and gave this warrior all his water and all his food, but then the warrior left him and disappeared into the blizzard.

"Wandering Shadow decided it was his time to die—" Davis paused. "Mokesh knew when it was his time to die. Do you think maybe all the Ndee do?"

"At one time, I believe they did," Bram said. "Now, though—" His words trailed off and he shrugged.

Again he'd surprised Vala with what he seemed to know about the Apache.

"Anyway," Davis went on, "instead of dying, Wandering Shadow found this shining lost pouch and knew he had to return it to Spirit Mountain. After he did that, he got one wish—a big wish, a thunder wish. On account of he was a wise old man, he wished his people wouldn't ever have to be cold or go hungry again. So do you know what he got for them?"

Vala shook her head.

Bram said, "I do, but this is your story to tell, not mine."

"The gift of the Great Spirit to the Ndee was the buffalo," Davis told them.

"I liked that story," Vala said.

Bram nodded. "That's what I mean about treasure. The buffalo were a greater treasure to Wandering Shadow's people than gold or jewels."

"Yeah, I guess they were," Davis agreed. "But they wouldn't be to me. I'd rather have gold any day." He looked at Vala. "Now it's your turn, Mom."

"I don't know any legends," Vala said. "And I've never been any good at making up stories."

"You could tell about when you were a little girl and lived in Arizona," Davis said. "You hardly ever talk about that."

"Sounds good to me," Bram chimed in.

Vala thought a moment. "Okay, I can come up with something about that time. Davis's story mentioned a thunder wish; mine'll be about rain."

"That leaves me lightning," Bram said.

"You can have lightning; there's only rain in mine." She paused, wondering how to begin. If it were only Davis there'd be no problem, but Bram would be listening, too. "Once upon a time," she finally began, "there was a little girl who wanted to dress up like a princess for a Halloween party her friend down the street was having.

"The little girl's mother didn't sew and her father thought buying a ready-made costume was a waste of money, so her mother taped together a white dress out of old leftover crepe paper stored in the attic. She trimmed it with gold fronds meant to decorate a Christmas tree. The little girl thought she was beautiful in the paper dress, especially after her mother curled her straight hair.

"As she walked down the block to the party house, it began to rain. Her pretty dress just sort of turned to mush and her curls disappeared, so she ran home crying.

"Her mother didn't have any more crepe paper, but she found a piece of black cloth. So she cut a hole in it for the little girl's head to go through, other holes for her arms and trimmed it off so it made a long dress. She braided the little girl's hair, made a pointed hat out of cardboard, colored it black with a crayon and told the little girl it had stopped raining and now she could go as a witch.

"The little girl didn't like that idea one bit. She was sure she looked awful and everyone would make fun of her. Then her father said, 'A princess is boring. A witch is interesting. Wouldn't you rather be interesting?'

"Well, she didn't know whether she would or not, but she went to the party as a witch. No one laughed at her and so she had a good time after all."

After a pause, Davis said, "Grandpa was right. I think witches are more interesting. For one thing, they get to turn people into frogs."

"While the poor, boring princess only gets to kiss the frog," Bram put in. "Ribbet," he croaked. That cracked Davis up.

"The best I can come up with is a story about something funny that happened while I was at law school," Bram said.

In her surprise, Vala blurted, "You're a lawyer?"

He shrugged. "I know everyone hates lawyers but someone has to do it."

"How come you're a guide, then?" Davis asked.

"Which would you rather be?" Bram countered.

"A guide!"

"So you've answered the question. It's like witching. Guiding is more interesting."

"For your story, I think I'd rather hear why you switched professions," Vala said. "You said yours would be about lightning—so how did it strike and change your mind?"

"It's not as funny as the law school incident."

"We don't care, do we, Davis?"

"I want the lightning story," Davis told him.

"You might say it all started off with a necktie," Bram began. "I happen to hate them. In Arizona you can usually get by with a bolo tie, but not in the courtroom. So I bought an expensive silk, very conservative, navy blue tie, learned how to put the correct knot in it and never unknotted it, just slipped it over my head until the next court case. Kept the thing in my blazer pocket, left the blazer hanging at the office.

"At the time my mother was making rag rugs

from old nylon stockings and panty hose and was always scrounging for them. So I asked the secretaries in the law firm I worked for to save their old hose for my mother's rugs. Came a day in court. The day before, one of the secretaries told me she'd brought me a pair of old black panty hose. I was busy at the time and told her to just stuff them somewhere out of sight.

"On the court day I'm running late, grab the blazer, put it on when I'm almost to the door of the court, reach in my pocket for the tie, slide it over my head and try to tighten it as I enter the courtroom. The judge, who's just been seated, stares straight at me, his eyebrows rising higher and higher.

"I fumble with the tie, can't find the knot. Not until the snickering starts do I realize what I've done." He paused. "Know what it was?"

"I bet that's where your secretary put her black panty hose," Davis said, snickering himself. "In your pocket."

Vala found the picture of Bram in a courtroom with panty hose draped around his neck irresistibly funny. She and Davis couldn't stop laughing.

"Got cited for contempt of court," Bram added. "Blasted judge had no sense of humor. That's when I decided it was entirely possible I might have picked the wrong profession."

After a time, Bram said, "When it rained at summer camp, we used to sing songs."

"Good idea," Vala told him. "How about 'You Are My Sunshine?' "

They started with that. Davis taught them a couple he'd learned in camp and they sang those and others, one after another until they grew hoarse. At that point Davis eased down and stretched out on his sleeping bag.

"Whatever happened to your guitar?" Vala asked Bram.

"I didn't realize you knew I had one," he said. "It's around somewhere."

"Can you still play it?" Davis asked.

"I suppose. Haven't tried lately."

"He was something in high school with that guitar," Vala said, remembering. "He knew all the right tunes and sometimes he'd play after classes out in the parking lot, standing there by his motorcycle, surrounded by a crowd."

Davis stared at him. "You had a Harley?"

"No such luck. An old Honda."

"Still . . ." Davis seemed lost in admiration.

"I never noticed you in any crowd," Bram said to Vala.

"I was there." She didn't add that she'd tried hard not to be obvious.

"Staying in the background seemed to be a characteristic of yours."

"I got over it." Wanting to shift attention from her, she said, "I never in my wildest guess would have imagined you as a lawyer."

"Nobody else's either. Could be that's why I took

prelaw when I got that college baseball scholarship and then went on to law school."

Vala expected Davis to chime in about now. When he didn't, she glanced at him and saw he'd fallen asleep.

Following her gaze, Bram said, "Should we be quiet?"

She smiled. "Never worry about waking Davis up. Ten brass bands marching by couldn't rouse him. He's the soundest sleeper in the world."

"He's a good kid. Smart, too."

"Unfortunately his father doesn't seem to know that. Or care. The only thing Davis could do to make Neal take any notice is to become an outstanding athlete. That's not likely."

"He interested in sports at all?"

"He likes to watch baseball but gave up on playing it after one season in Little League. Davis is not well-coordinated, no matter how hard he practices. Lately he's given up completely on trying to please his father. I can't blame him, since nothing does."

Bram scowled but remained quiet, seemingly lost in his own thoughts. "Hell of thing for a kid to go through," he said finally. "Shouldn't happen."

"You know that and I know that, but try to tell Neal."

"Why'd you marry him?"

Taken by surprise, she blurted, "Because he asked me." After a moment, she realized, to her distress, that it might actually be the truth. She hadn't been in love with Neal, no matter how she'd tried to convince herself she was.

Bram shook his head.

"Okay, so it was a lousy reason," she snapped. "I'm sure he's much happier with his new wife and son."

"How about you?"

She shrugged. "I'm happier without him. So is Davis, actually. He no longer has to hear on a daily basis how he doesn't measure up."

"Man's a fool not to be proud of a kid like Davis. Take the old Ndee he befriended. Mokesh saw something in Davis that made him believe in the boy's potential or he'd never have given Davis so much of his time, much less that map. It's not easy to impress an old medicine man."

"I thought Mr. Mokesh was probably just lonely."

"With others to talk to in that nursing home, he chose Davis. You can bet it wasn't as simple as loneliness."

"I've noticed you seem to know quite a lot about Mr. Mokesh's people. Like Davis, you don't say Apache; you say Ndee."

"Everything has its right name."

She waited for him to go on before finally realizing that was the only answer she was likely to get.

"It was good of you to offer Davis a kitten," she said into the silence, "but I don't know if we'll be able to take it home with us."

"Let's wait and see. I can always ship it." He shifted position on his sleeping bag to peer at the rain through the little view window on the flap. "Isn't letting up any yet."

His new position brought them closer together but she hesitated to shift herself, not wanting him to think his nearness disturbed her. Which it did. He seemed to radiate a sensual aura.

She found the weather a safe subject. "No more lightning and thunder, though. The rain can't last forever."

He nodded, then said, "Surprised me when you mentioned my guitar. I'd have sworn you never noticed me that much back then."

Never noticed him! When she'd spent every school day waiting for a glimpse of Bram, hoping and praying he'd say even one word to her. "You were pretty hard to miss," she said dryly.

"Always in trouble, you mean."

"That, too. Come on, Bram. You were a bigger-than-life rebel. Everyone in the entire school paid attention to what you did, students and staff alike. Plus you were the star of our winning baseball team."

"I figure that's the only reason those in power put up with me. We rebels have to have at least one in, you know."

Vala smiled at him. She'd always found Bram sexy but she'd never dreamed he'd turn out to be fun. "I didn't know you'd won that scholarship, though."

"Got it when the university recruited me. I decided to accept it—what did I have to lose?

"So you wound up with a law degree you don't use."

"Not a total loss. I still use a lot of what I learned getting it. And who can predict the future? That degree may come in handy someday."

"At least you had the courage to know what you really wanted."

He gave her a lopsided smile. "Maybe, maybe not. In some areas, though, I think maybe I always knew what I wanted. Trouble was, I didn't know how to get it. Figure that's how the idea of law school came in to begin with."

Vala sighed. "I don't think I ever knew what I really wanted. If I had, I wouldn't have married Neal. But then, of course, I wouldn't have Davis. He's the prize I never expected."

The tent seemed to have gotten smaller, she thought. Which was impossible. Yet Bram's nearness was overwhelming her. She struggled to find words to throw up as a barrier between them.

"Surely at one time you must have thought of marrying," she said.

"Nope. No reason to."

"How about being in love?"

"Who knows what love is?"

"I'm the last person to ask," she said tartly.

"You brought it up. Weren't you ever in love with misguided Neal?"

She shook her head, ashamed to admit it aloud.

You ought to love the man you married, shouldn't you?

Time to shift the focus back to him. "You could have had your pick of any girl in high school, so I imagine—"

He cut her off. "You're wrong."

Vala stared at him. "I don't think so. Remember, I was in that school, watching and listening. What I was trying to say, though, is if you've never fallen in love or married, it surely hasn't been for lack of opportunity."

"Rebels don't make good marital partners."

"If by that you mean women don't understand them . . ."

"Don't mean that. I mean rebels can't be counted on to be there."

His tone was so bitter that she began to understand he must be speaking of someone other than himself.

"Been there, done that," he added. "Not again."

It occurred to her that in high school he'd lived alone with his mother. Was he talking about his absent father? Whatever it was, she decided Bram had been hurt as a child. Without thinking, she reached out and placed her hand over his in a gesture of sympathy.

Though she hadn't seen him move, suddenly he seemed a lot closer.

"Invitation?" he asked, watching her.

"I—um—" She couldn't find words to tell him no. And then it was too late.

His mouth brushed against hers in a feather kiss, which shouldn't have been the slightest bit erotic. Or at least that's what she tried to tell herself as she leaned into the kiss, helpless to deny the very real invitation she was now offering.

His arms came around her, pulling her close, his lips urging surrender as he deepened the kiss. No man, certainly not Neal, had ever aroused her so completely by one kiss. She wanted to melt against him, melt into him, to possess and be possessed. The feeling was completely foreign to her, making her realize there'd been a pitiful lack in her life up until now.

If this was a prelude, she wasn't sure she'd live through the main performance. She was so consumed with longing she could hardly think straight.

Wrapped in his arms, his male scent drugging her senses, the taste of his mouth branding her, she had no desire to try to free herself because it felt as though she belonged exactly where she was.

She couldn't tell herself the reason for her eager response was that she hadn't let any man kiss her for a very long time because, the truth was, no man had ever kissed her like this. It was even possible no other man could, only Bram.

"Long overdue," he murmured against her mouth without letting her go.

He was right. More than ten years overdue, if only he knew it.

FIVE

Vala, held close in Bram's arms, never wanted to leave them, not until she began to realize where she was. Closed in a tent on the side of a mountain during a storm. With her son asleep only a few feet away. Not that they'd done anything really improper, but she'd come close to getting swept away by her feelings.

Bram's words about the rain rushing down the mountain trail in a torrent echoed in her head. She repeated them aloud as she freed herself. "It doesn't do to get swept away."

He let her go without a fuss. Easing back so he was sitting once again on his own sleeping bag, he said, "Why not?"

Flustered, she gestured at Davis, still sleeping peacefully.

Bram grinned at her. "So if we're alone, it's okay?"

"No! What I mean is—" She paused, unsure of what she actually did mean.

"Took me by surprise, too," he admitted.

She wondered if he meant her admittedly ardent response or that he'd been in danger of getting swept away, too. "I don't usually—" she began, then hesitated. Kiss strange men? Bram wasn't exactly a stranger. "I mean, I shouldn't have let it happen," she finished lamely.

"You had a choice?"

Bram was teasing her, but at the same time trying to force the issue. If he'd read her body language right, she'd no more been in control once they got into that zinger of a kiss than he'd been. He was damned if he was going to let her negate what had happened.

"There's always a choice," she snapped.

"What you mean is you finally remembered Davis was asleep in the tent with us."

Vala flushed.

Aha. Struck home. He pushed on. "We can't ignore what's between us. Tell me you haven't felt the pull ever since we met again in that Apache Junction cafe."

She took a deep breath and let it out slowly. "I've never forgotten the last time I saw you, years before. How could you have been so cruel?"

He stared at her, completely baffled. "Cruel? Me? What the devil are you talking about? You think it wasn't cruel for you to stand there that night looking down your nose at me as though I'd just crawled out from under a rock?"

She gave him an incredulous look. "I did no

such thing! I knew why you were there and I was trying not to cry—that's what really happened."

"Knew why I was there?" His words echoed his confusion.

"You should have been ashamed of yourself!"

"Why? What did I do? Nothing, that's what."

"It was mean. I thought you'd never noticed how I watched you in school, how I hung around on the fringes of your crowd. But you must have. Otherwise you wouldn't have come to my house that night. One of your buddies must have told you my parents weren't home."

"Hell, they bowled in a couple's league every Thursday night. It didn't take a Mensa member to turn that up. I didn't have a clue you even knew who I was. But I sure as hell was interested in you. Took me a long time to make a move."

"I wouldn't have cared if it had been *your* move." Her voice rose. "Instead what did you do?"

He scowled. "Since you seem to have some secret information I don't possess—what *did* I do?"

"You made a bet!" Her voice broke on the last word and she turned her face from him.

Bram blinked, taken aback. "What in hell are you talking about? What bet?"

"Don't deny it. I overheard two of your buddies talking about how they'd bet you couldn't get so much as a kiss out of the Ice Maiden. Then the same night you show up at my house after never so much as saying one word ever to me at school."

"I vaguely remember the bet," Bram said after

a moment or two. "But what makes you think anyone ever called you the Ice Maiden?"

Vala turned toward him again, frowning. "What
are you saying?"

"Honey, you tried so hard to blend into the walls
that you didn't even have a nickname, good or bad.
The Ice Maiden was Lori Salter. I may have
showed up at your house hoping for a kiss, but it
was my own idea. The truth is, you fascinated me,
but I figured you'd never go out with me. So I
didn't talk to you at school for fear of having everyone watch you turn me down."

"But—but—" she sputtered.

"You were so far off with that bet business you
weren't even on the planet."

"Are you telling me the truth about Lori Salter?"

"Want to ask me if I won the bet?"

"No! Now that I think about it, Lori *was* sort of
standoffish. I suppose . . ." She let the words trail
off.

"Tell you anyway. I kissed her, all right. Winning
the bet was a lot more fun than the kiss."

She slanted him a quelling glance.

"I didn't even come close to kissing you that
night," he said. "Didn't so much as get one kind
word, as I recall."

"I wanted you to kiss me!" she cried. "But not
on a bet. I spent the whole time you were there
trying not to burst into tears."

He shook his head. "I didn't have a clue. Between us, we blew it. I guess the only remedy is to try to make up for lost time."

"I think we already have," she said.

"Wrong. We've hardly begun." He gave her a long, speculative look. "If you hadn't been hung up on that bet and I *had* kissed you that night, I wonder what it would have been like?"

"We can hardly go back and find out."

He persisted. "Would you have responded?"

"What do you think?"

He ran his forefinger along the curve of her lower lip. "I think we'd still have been locked together in that kiss when your parents got home and there'd have been hell to pay."

She bit his finger.

"How come you're biting him, Mom?" Davis asked sleepily.

"Because I've been teasing her," Bram said before Vala could speak.

"Oh." Davis sat up. "Hey, I don't hear the rain hitting the tent anymore. Is the storm over?"

Bram's gaze caught Vala's. "Is it?" he asked.

She eased over to the flap window and looked out.

"All over," she said, glancing at Bram. "The sun's out."

Though there were hours of daylight left, Bram opted to stay where they were, give the horses a good rubdown and let the tent have a chance to dry in the sun's warmth.

Vala watched as he let Davis build their small campfire, which sputtered and smoked because of the wet. "Be careful," she called to her son, earning an exasperated look from him. It was kind of Bram to let Davis do things, but she sometimes felt he didn't realize the boy was only nine.

The thunder and lightning were past, the rain gone, but not her inner turmoil. Seeing Bram and Davis huddle over the old map, she marveled at what that ancient scrap of deerskin had led her into. An ambush? At the moment, it almost felt like that.

She wasn't ready for any of this, wasn't ready to discover she was wrong about their last meeting. She found herself in completely unknown territory, as dangerous in its way as the Superstitions.

Neal had taught her that men couldn't be trusted. After the divorce she'd decided it was safer not to get involved with any other man, which had been easy up until now. The problem was, Bram couldn't be put in the just any other man category. He was someone she found much too attractive and she was trapped in his company for the next few days. Luckily Davis was with them. But would he be buffer enough?

She carried her worried confusion to bed with her that evening and sleep didn't come easily.

Bram, outside under the stars, studied the very slightly lopsided moon and decided it'd be full in two days. He fell into a reverie about making love to Vala under mountain moonlight, managing to get himself completely aroused.

He shut down the erotic imaginings. Just where the devil do you think you're going to take this? he asked himself.

Sure, he wanted her, but Vala was no quick fix. Would she expect more than a night or two of pleasure? Would she understand that when she flew back east chances were they'd never see one another again? For that matter, would she even let him near her in the first place?

Smiling as he recalled her eager response to his kiss, he decided if the right time and place came together, they'd go up together like rockets. One question remained—was that the smart way to take it? He wasn't ready to get seriously tangled up with any woman, maybe never would be.

He fell asleep before he found an answer.

Nothing went well in the morning. For a start, the oatmeal burned. Then it looked like the pack-horse had gone lame, though digging a pebble out of the left hind hoof seemed to help.

Vala insisted on trying to saddle Susie Q by herself and wound up with the saddle sliding under the mare's belly. Vala snapped at Bram when he tried to help, so he let Davis show her.

Before they mounted up, a brightly colored gila monster, in all its beaded glory, darted into the camp area. When it stopped temporarily on a rock, Davis hunkered down over it, fascinated. Bram was watching to see he didn't get too close when Vala finally spotted the lizard.

"Get away!" she screamed at Davis. "It's poisonous. It'll bite you."

Davis backed off with a scowl. There was none of his cheerful chatter after that. When they finally set off, they made a silent crew.

At the first rest stop, Bram took Vala aside. "Don't hover over the kid," he said in a low tone, making sure Davis couldn't hear. "He's capable of thinking for himself—let him."

"I suppose you wanted him bitten by that poisonous lizard."

"I had an eye on him; he was in no danger."

She glared at him. "Davis is only nine."

Bram shrugged and walked away. The boy wasn't his; he'd done the best he could to loosen the apron strings. But it seemed to him that as Davis learned competence at different camp chores, he was beginning to realize he wasn't what his father thought of him—useless. She ought to encourage her son's independence.

They stopped to eat at noon at a relatively flat area that branched off in several directions. When Davis started to explore, Vala warned him to be careful of the cacti and to watch out for snakes. With some difficulty, Bram kept his mouth shut.

"Aw, Mom, I'm just trying to spot the bear,"

Davis grumbled. "We need to find it for a landmark."

"Okay, but don't go out of sight."

Didn't she realize her kid was about as dependable as any nine-year-old boy could be? Bram wondered. And didn't she remember how repeated warnings made a kid want to rebel? He shrugged. Maybe she hadn't been as ornery in their younger days as he'd been.

After Davis returned, they ate, remounted and went on. Bram wanted to reach another plateau a couple of miles along the trail to set up their night camp, so he kept a steady pace. He wondered what she'd do when darkness mantled the mountain. Davis usually went into the tent early and so there'd be just the two of them under the stars.

Unless she made the first move, best to let things be until she was ready to take their relationship further. He began whistling an old song that had a line in it about a kiss just being a kiss.

From her position at the rear, Vala recognized the tune and recalled enough of the words to decide it was directed at her. She glared at Bram's back. That damn kiss aside, where did he get off telling her how to raise her son? He didn't have any kids; what did he know about it?

She worked hard at trying not to be an overprotective mother and she resented being told she was. If she didn't take care of Davis, who would?

Later, after they reached the spot where their night camp was to be, Vala found that Bram had taken her at her word when she'd told him she'd take care of Susie Q from now on. He and Davis got the gear off their horses in what seemed to her an impossibly fast speed, rubbed the animals down, fed and left them—and her—while she was still struggling with the mare's saddle.

She could hear them laughing as they set up the tent. At her? Hey, she wanted to call, it's not easy being a tenderfoot. At least I'm trying to pull my weight. But her annoyance faded as she realized her son had laughed more in the past few days than he had in the last six months. Bram was good for him, too.

Where had that "too" come from? Did she really think Bram was good for her? A man whose kiss had her melting like candle wax in the sun?

By the time she'd finished with Susie Q, they had the tent up and were working together to start supper.

As they ate, Vala decided the problem with camp food was that the limited selection made meals somewhat boring. Not that she'd dream of saying so. Though no gourmet chef, with a full refrigerator, shelves of supplies and a modern stove, plus microwave, she could cook a decent meal now.

After they were through eating, Bram served up his usual warning for dessert, a different one each time, about avoiding harm in the great Arizona outdoors.

"So a pair of pliers should be a part of every camper's gear," he finished. "Because of the fishhook end of cacti spines, you need something more substantial than tweezers to pull them out."

"A kid at my summer camp got a fishhook caught in his leg," Davis said. "He sure yelled when the nurse pulled it out."

She wondered if her son retained any of Bram's cautionary desert teachings. It was hard to tell what impressed a nine-year-old and what didn't. Which was why she often repeated her warnings to Davis. She did *not* hover over him; she was merely being careful.

As night closed in around them and the moon rose, Davis was the first to opt for the tent. Vala told herself she'd give him enough time to get undressed and fall asleep and then she'd call it a day as well. Not that she was especially tired, but it was only prudent to avoid being alone with Bram.

"No more aches and pains?" he asked her.

She shook her head. "I guess I'm turning into a real horsewoman."

"I suppose. Too bad." He grinned at her. "I got to looking forward to our liniment sessions."

"You're incorrigible."

"No, ma'am, just an opportunist."

With the feel of his hands massaging her bare skin all too easy to remember, Vala decided retreat was the better part of valor. She faked a yawn.

"Ready to run off scared?" Bram asked.

She started to put on an indignant act, then gave it up as stupid. "Something of the sort, yes."

"No need. It's your call."

"My call? You expect me to—to—" She couldn't find the right words.

"To discover what you want?" He nodded.

"Are you that sure of yourself?"

"Nope. Hope springs eternal."

Despite herself, she smiled and relaxed. Even with the sensual awareness arcing between them, Bram was easy to be with.

"I wish I hadn't misunderstood your visit years ago," she said. "We might have become friends."

"Yeah—*good* friends."

Though she was aware it wouldn't have happened if her parents could have found any way to prevent Bram from coming near their daughter, she went on picturing her timid teenage self and brash Bram together.

"The kids at school would have had their socks knocked off when they saw me riding on the back of your bike," she said.

He chuckled. "I'd like to have seen that myself. You wouldn't have been too scared?"

She shook her head. "Not if I was with you."

He reached over and covered her hand with his. "You actually trusted the guy I was then?"

Turning her hand over, she clasped his. "I had a bad case of hero worship."

His grip tightened. "Wish I'd known. What about now?"

"I don't know," she said honestly. "Being with you confuses me. I'll admit there's something between us, but I'm not sure I want to explore it."

"There's an old sixties song about regretting the path not taken."

"I realize I may regret it if I don't. But even worse, what if I regret it if I do?"

"Why would you?"

She sighed, enjoying the sensation of her hand resting safely in his. But there'd be nothing safe about allowing herself to see where the path with Bram would take her.

"Maybe men don't experience loss in the same way women do," she said finally. "Neal is the only man I've known really well and I doubt that he's ever had such a feeling."

Bram released her hand, saying gruffly, "I'm not Neal."

"I'm not comparing you!"

"Oh, yes, you are. You have been from the moment I walked into that cafe."

About to come up with an indignant denial, she realized there was some truth in his words and she smiled at him. "Guilty. And don't you wish you knew how favorably you stack up?"

That earned her a raised eyebrow. "Favorably?"

"You'd make a far better father than he ever could be," she said.

"Judging by what you've told me, sounds like almost any man would."

"You *care*. Not only about how Davis feels but about other things. You have no idea how your voice softened when you mentioned your cat and her kittens. And you were kind enough to try to ease my aches, even though you were annoyed that I'd lied about being able to ride. You don't treat the horses like dumb animals, either."

"But you figure you're going to be left unhappier than you are now if we make love."

Vala sighed again. "I'm afraid of that, yes."

He offered her a lopsided smile. "So much for the staying power of hero worship."

If only she could close her mind to any doubt and fling herself into his arms, where she was aching to be.

"Except for the lie about riding, you're the most honest woman I've ever met," Bram told her. "Wrongheaded but honest."

"So are you. Honest, I mean. Not feeding me any lies about wonderful tomorrows or everlasting love. Amazing in a man."

"Here's my take. We want each other. Neither of us can tell now what will happen after that, if anything. You're afraid to find out. I'm not."

"I came out here to search for treasure that probably doesn't exist," she said. "I never dreamed I'd run into you."

"What you'll find—besides me, and I'm no treasure—all depends on how you define the word. I keep trying to teach Davis that treasure isn't necessarily something tangible."

"That's a difficult concept for a kid. I hope he won't be too disappointed."

"Don't underestimate your son's intelligence. And don't underestimate your own courage, either."

After a pause he added, "It's time for me to kiss you good night and send you to your tent."

Before she could object, he leaned to her and captured her mouth with his. Instead of the fiery passion of their first kiss, this one was soft and gentle. But under the sweetness lay a throbbing current of need that she sensed in him, even as she felt it herself.

He pulled away. "Dream of me," he ordered.

As Vala undressed in her tent and crawled into her sleeping bag, his command echoed in her mind. I won't, she told herself firmly. Isn't it enough he's invaded my every thought? I refuse to let him into my dreams.

Unfortunately, once she was asleep, she couldn't command her unconscious mind. . . .

She and Bram raced across the country on a big Harley—what bikers call a hog. Clinging to him as they flew down a lonesome desert highway, she relished the feel of the wind blowing past. To either side of the road, bright patches of red dotted the barrenness—flowers of the ocotillo, she knew, bloomed in May.

But this wasn't May—was it?

She brushed away the sense of wrongness. What could be more right than fleeing with Bram on his bike?

Fleeing? From what?

Unease threatened her contentment. Was there something important she'd forgotten? Left behind? Yet what could be more important than Bram?

He was taking her away from loneliness, from boredom, taking them into a fantasy realm of happiness for just the two of them. Once they reached this fabulous spot, he'd wrap his arms around her and never let her go. They'd never return, the two of them would dwell forever in that magic place.

If only this feeling she was forgetting something would vanish, she'd be blissfully happy. . . .

SIX

When Vala awoke in the morning, the dream was still haunting her. It took her a few moments to realize that Davis wasn't in the tent, which didn't alarm her. On this trip he'd almost always been up and about before she roused. As she dressed, she thought about the dream and suddenly realized Davis hadn't been in it, any more than he was in the tent. He was what she'd left behind. Something she'd never do.

Shaking her head, she emerged from the tent and glanced around. The day was fair and slightly cool. Neither Davis nor Bram were in sight. She poured herself a cup of coffee and sipped at it while she breathed in the fresh mountain air.

When, from behind her, Bram said, "Good morning," she almost dropped the cup.

"You scared me half to death, sneaking up behind me like that," she accused.

"Not intentional. Davis sleeping in?"

She gaped at him for a moment, belatedly aware

her son was still nowhere in sight. "He wasn't with you?"

Bram shook his head. "Haven't seen him at all this morning. You mean he's not in the tent?"

"No!"

As one they turned to look at the horses. All four were still tethered.

"He's lost!" Vala cried. "He's lost up here with poisonous snakes and lizards all around. He could have fallen off a cliff or . . ."

"Calm down," Bram told her. "Where we are now there are no cliffs he could fall off. And he knows about poisonous reptiles. My guess is he went exploring while he was waiting for us to get up."

"But you sleep outside. You must have seen him."

"I slept later than usual."

"Do something, can't you?" she demanded. "My son's lost on this cactus-infested mountain and you stand there telling me to calm down." She cupped her hands around her mouth and shouted, "Davis!"

An echo was the only reply.

"We've got to find him before it's too late," she said. "I'll go this way and you go that." She started off.

His hand gripped her arm, stopping her. "I run this outfit." His voice was flat and hard. "I give the orders. We don't split up. I repeat: We *do not* split up. First thing you know there'd be two lost people instead of one. And I don't mean me."

Panic rose in Vala. Wasn't he going to do anything? "He's only nine," she reminded him.

"Davis has been to summer camps. And he's listened to my reminders of what to do if you get lost. It may take a little time, but we'll find him."

"Your reminders!" She flung the words at him. "I can barely recall whatever advice you gave. If I was lost and scared I wouldn't remember a word."

"Davis isn't you. I have faith in the kid." He knelt, eased something from a pack and slid it into his pocket. "Okay, follow me and we'll do a widening circle search. He can't be far off."

"Then why didn't he answer me when I called him?" she demanded as she trotted after him, trying to keep up with his long strides.

"Sounds carry differently in the mountains." He shouted Davis's name. Again, nothing.

"It's all your fault," she said, beside herself with worried apprehension. What if Davis was lying somewhere hurt?

"It's no one's fault. Davis got an early start, maybe on purpose, while I wasn't awake to see him take off from camp."

"What do you mean on purpose?"

"That early, neither of us was around to stop him and so he probably figured it was an ideal time to go look for the bear. Kids always think they can find their way back. For him it'll be a lesson learned the hard way."

"He must be scared to death. And maybe hurt."

"Don't borrow trouble."

Easy for him to say, she thought resentfully as they started another, wider circling. Davis wasn't *his* son. She called Davis's name again, the uncaring echo sending a shiver down her spine. She pictured him rushing this way and that and getting more and more lost as he moved farther and farther away from the camp.

As if reading her mind, Bram took care of that scenario by saying, "He won't be far away. Once he realizes he's lost, he'll stop and stay in one spot."

Vala remembered that not moving was one of the things Bram had emphasized. But how could he expect a scared kid to dredge that up?

"Davis!" Bram bellowed.

Mixed in with the echo, Vala thought she heard something else. "Listen!" she cried.

"I hear him." Bram stopped and turned his head in one direction, then the other. "That way," he said, pointing.

They found Davis with tearstained cheeks, huddled against a rock. But when Vala rushed to hug him, he backed away, warning, "Don't touch me. I'm full of stickers."

She held, belatedly noticing the cactus spines sticking through his clothes. "Oh, my poor b—" She caught herself before "baby" slipped past and humiliated him. "Poor Davis," she said.

"I did what you said," Davis told Bram. "I stayed put." He sniffed and wiped his face with a grimy hand. "I should've stopped where I was sooner, but I got scared about being lost and that's how come I stumbled into the cactus."

"You're a brave kid," Bram said. "Not everyone would have calmed down and remembered to stay in one place. Especially after getting stabbed with all those spines." He pulled a pair of pliers from his pocket. "Brought these along, just in case."

Most of the spines were on the backs of Davis's legs and in his behind, so Vala was able to let him lean against her while Bram went to work.

"They all have to come out or they fester," Bram warned. "And it'll hurt when I yank them free—can't help that. You can yell if you want, nobody around to hear but me and your mom and we know it's painful. I'd yell if someone was doing this to me."

"Screaming's more my style," Vala put in, knowing the worst thing she could do for Davis was to start weeping over the pain he must be feeling, pain that would get worse while the spines were being pulled out.

She steeled herself not to wince as Bram gripped the first one with the jaws of the pliers.

"Ow!" Davis cried as Bram yanked it out.

By the time every spine had been pulled from his skin, Davis was unabashedly crying. Vala gathered him into her arms, being careful not to touch the sore spots.

Bram hunkered down to the boy's level, put a

hand on his shoulder and murmured, "You did good, partner."

After a time, Davis pushed away from Vala and swiped a hand across his face. "It hurt a lot," he muttered.

"Yup," Bram agreed. "What we have to do next is get you to Pauline's. It's not far, but you'll have to walk. Think you're up to it?"

About to ask why they couldn't ride, Vala realized Davis must be too sore to sit on a horse.

"I guess so," Davis said uncertainly. "Who's Pauline?"

"She's a Superstition Mountain hermit, and not the only one around, either. Lucky for us, she knows me and will let us in because she's a medicine woman and can help those spine stab wounds of yours heal a lot faster than they would otherwise."

"They won't hurt so much?"

"You got it. So if you can make it to Pauline's, you'll soon be feeling better."

Back at the camp, Bram and Vala stowed the gear and, with each of them leading two horses, with Davis they picked their way on foot up a rocky slope and into a wide crevasse. Set into the crevasse was a rickety-looking cabin perched on a bed of boulders.

"Is Pauline a real medicine woman?" Davis asked. By now he was limping, but he hadn't complained "A Ndee, I mean."

"No one's sure what she is or where she came from, but she's a medicine woman, all right."

Davis looked at Vala. "Is it okay if I call her Pauline?"

"No one ever calls her anything else," Bram said.

"Then I guess you can, too," Vala told her son.

Bram stopped a fair distance from the cabin, cupped his hands together and blew into them, making a strange wailing sound. He then waited until the cabin door opened and a tall, thin woman appeared on the tiny porch holding something that looked to Vala like a shotgun. She caught her breath.

"Bram Hunter," he called. "Got a hurt boy here."

The woman waved them on toward her cabin.

"Are you sure it's safe?" Vala asked in a low tone.

"She'd have shot over our heads by now if she didn't want us here," Bram said. "She might turn me away sometimes, but she'd never deny help to a child. Pauline's kindhearted."

Maybe, but the woman also carried a shotgun. Still, if she could help Davis, that was all-important.

"Don't offer to pay her," Bram warned before they got to the cabin. "You'll insult her. I'll tell her we'll arrange for supplies to be sent to her when we get back down the mountain. She won't say yes, but she won't refuse."

"That's like barter," Davis said unexpectedly. "We learned about barter in school. She gives me some medicine and you guys give her some supplies."

"Right again, partner," Bram told him.

Up closer, Vala saw the cabin was made of planks and metal haphazardly clobbered together. The roof appeared to be sheets of tin.

"Used to be a prospector's cabin in the old days," Bram said. "After he died it was abandoned until Pauline moved in and fixed it up some."

"A prospector for gold?" Davis asked.

"Yup. He couldn't've found much, to judge by the looks of the cabin."

"Maybe he hid what he found, like the Lost Dutchman Mine."

Bram shrugged. "By all accounts, he died flat broke, like the Dutchman."

By now they were almost to the porch and the woman standing there obviously overheard the last remarks because she said, "Crazy men. These mountains keep their gold."

Pauline's voice was surprisingly melodious, in contrast to her stark appearance. Two dark braids, streaked with gray, fell almost to her waist. She wore a long brown dress that looked as though it might be made from homespun cloth, with a deerskin vest over it.

Vala couldn't begin to guess her age, though she had to be at least sixty.

"I got stuck by a cactus," Davis told Pauline before anyone else could speak. "Bram says you can heal up the holes. I sure like your headband.

Mokesh had one, but his was sort of worn out."
Davis winced as he climbed the porch steps.

Pauline smiled at him. "Mokesh, is it? We'll talk
about him later, after you feel better. First things
first."

"I'm Vala and he's my son, Davis," Vala said,
stepping onto the porch, trying not to notice the
shotgun, now leaning against the cabin. "I'm
pleased to meet you, Pauline."

"Ain't nobody said that to me and meant it for
quite a spell," Pauline told her.

"I believe you can help Davis," Vala said, putting
as much conviction into her voice as possible.

"Looks like maybe you brung me some good
ones," Pauline said to Bram. She picked up the
shotgun and led the way into the cabin.

Because the several windows were small, the
one-room interior was dark but, Vala saw, clean and
neat. The furniture consisted of wooden chairs and
a table, plus a cot. A curtained alcove held, she
supposed, a bed and, perhaps a dresser. One entire
wall was taken up by shelved open cupboards, with
a sink fitted into one of the cupboards. Plastic
water bottles were lined up on the lower shelves.
The stove appeared to be either butane or oil.

In one corner was a stone fireplace with a very
small fire burning. The place smelled of herbs.

"You got a cool house," Davis said as Pauline
led him to the cot.

"It suits," she said. "Now you got to take all
your clothes off."

"Right in front of everyone?"

"If that bothers you, I'll herd us all onto the porch till you're under that sheet on the cot, flat on your belly."

"Maybe if you just turned your backs, you and Bram and Mom."

When Davis was ready, Vala watched as Pauline swung out a large kettle that hung over the fire and poured steaming water into a basin before she swung the kettle back into position.

"I ain't gonna scald the boy," Pauline said, evidently catching Vala's worried expression. "Might be best if you and Bram go set up your tent nearby while I take care of Davis."

"Good idea." Bram took Vala's hand, urging her out through the door.

"I don't know—" she began as he closed the door behind them.

"I do. Pauline won't do anything to harm Davis. Her potions will ease him and help healing. They're natural herbs. I don't have anything in my first-aid kit that'll work as well as what she'll do."

Vala glanced at the closed door, then sighed and followed Bram down the steps. What she really wanted to do was hover over her son, just as Bram had accused her of doing. Was it so wrong? Still, if Davis had wanted her to stay, he'd have asked her to.

She recalled that the last time he'd been to the doctor, he hadn't wanted her to come into the examining room with him. Somehow she'd have to adjust to the fact her little boy was growing up.

Once they'd set up the tent and made sure the horses were tethered and fed, Vala faced Bram.

"I'm sorry," she said. "I shouldn't have blamed you for Davis getting lost. I was too upset to think straight."

He nodded. "I took that under consideration. The boy's smarter than maybe you realize. Courageous, too. You've got a good kid there, Vala."

"I know. If only—" She sighed and didn't go on. If only was no more than a dream because Neal would never change, never recognize his son's worth.

Evidently following her train of thought, Bram said, "There's more to life than organized sports. Davis has excellent balance. I bet he'd be good on skis. Has he ever tried skiing?"

"No."

"Might be the place to start building his confidence in himself."

"You've been doing a fine job of that," she said. "I really do appreciate it. Acceptance from a man means so much to him."

"I didn't get much of that when I was a kid."

If she'd remembered rightly about Bram living with his mother only, then he must have had an absent father. No wonder he understood Davis so well.

Time to change the subject, Bram told himself. She didn't want to hear about his past problems.

"I'll lay odds Davis is not only comfortable by now, but asleep."

"I hope so."

He nodded toward the cabin. "If I'm right, then Pauline won't throw us out again. Come on."

He'd hit it on the button. Davis, lying on his stomach, was sound asleep on the cot. Bram listened as Vala explained to Pauline that Davis didn't wake easily so there was no need to be particularly quiet.

"I been waiting to tell you if you put that boy on a horse tomorrow you'll undo all the good that's got started," Pauline said in her deep, melodious voice. "He'd best stay right here for one more day."

"We'll do whatever you say," Bram told her.

"Good. 'Cause I need some roots and plants you two can fetch for me before dark. Gonna tell you right where they can be found. Lots quicker getting there with horses than on shank's mare, like me."

"We'll be glad to help out," Vala told her.

" 'Course you will. Couldn't be raising a fine boy like your son if you wasn't all right yourself."

Pauline eyed Bram. "Might be some rabbit stew on the fire when you get back. Old feller from the back of nowhere brought me a couple real early this morning."

Bram knew the rabbits must be payment for one of Pauline's remedies. "I'll take right kindly to that stew," he told her, grinning.

"Always making fun," she grumbled. "Get you going or the boy and me might just finish all that stew before you get back here. Here's the directions."

He listened while she told him what she wanted and how to get where the plants grew; then he took the trowel, clippers and basket she handed him.

Vala took another look at Davis before they went out.

"He'll do without you for a time," Pauline assured her. "Might be somebody else'd appreciate your attention, though. Providing he deserves it."

Bram put his hand over his heart. "I'm a most deserving man."

Pauline snorted. "They all say that." She fixed her attention on Vala and added, "He's better'n some."

On that note he and Vala left the cabin. Not until the horses were saddled and they'd mounted—Vala could now swing onto Susie Q like a pro, he noted—did he speak.

"How deserving do *you* think I am?"

"More than some," she said, imitating Pauline. "I've never had rabbit stew, by the way. How is it?"

"Anything Pauline cooks is good."

"I don't know how she can live as she does—so isolated and alone."

"I do. I have the tendency myself once in awhile."

She stared at him. "I guess I like people around too much to understand hermits."

He half-smiled. "I'm no hermit, though I admit the genes may be there."

"Genes?"

"My father was a wanderer. Or at least that's what my mother always called it." Inwardly, he cursed himself. What was there about this woman that made him want to dump the past on her, to tell her more than she'd want to know, more than he'd ever told anyone?

Abruptly, he shifted to something else. "Want to try sleeping under the stars tonight?" he asked. "There's going to be a penultimate moon."

"What kind of a moon is that?"

"My term for one night short of full. Hard to tell the difference, actually."

"Never in my life have I slept outside."

"Past time to try it, then." He didn't understand why he needed to share the experience with Vala, but he did. He wanted her to feel what he did—the awesome beauty of the night and the stars and the universe.

"If I can reserve the right to retreat to my tent," she said.

"You won't want to." He glanced up at the sky, all but devoid of clouds, and saw a hawk circling in a thermal.

Vala followed his gaze. "Isn't he gorgeous? I've sometimes wondered why predators so often are. Eagles, cougars, wolves—all graceful and deadly."

"They're doing what they were born to do—hunt for food. Like men used to in the old days. The

Ndee were never in one place long enough to grow crops—hunters, all of them."

"I can't think they found much to hunt in the Superstitions."

"There's game here. But the Ndee didn't trespass much on their sacred mountain."

"Have you studied the Ndee? You seem to know them well."

"Something like that."

No matter what subject they started out with, the conversation seemed to circle back to his past. No doubt because it was so easy to talk to Vala that he forgot to be careful what he said.

"Oh, look!" she cried, pointing. "That must be the landmark."

Bram looked, then turned to grin at her. "You spotted the guide bear, all right."

"I can't wait to tell Davis, but I hope he won't be too disappointed he wasn't the first to see the bear."

"Look at it this way. If he hadn't gotten lost and blundered into that cactus, we wouldn't have come to Pauline's and we wouldn't be where we are now. So Davis can take part of the credit."

"Wounded but justified," she said, smiling at him.

"Interesting. Old Mokesh's map has been accurate so far," Bram said. "The bear isn't as well known a landmark as the lizard. I knew roughly where it was, but not exactly. We'll have to change direction some when we hit the trail again."

"Do you actually think we might find something when we reach the map's end?"

"If you mean treasure, I doubt we'll find gold."

She sighed. "There has to be something. Davis will be heartbroken otherwise. He trusted Mokesh, so he believes in that map."

"Mokesh was a medicine man; Davis won't be disappointed." Bram wasn't sure how he knew this, but, as though Mokesh himself was whispering into his ear, he had no doubt he was right.

"Davis trusts you, too," she said.

Bram was well aware of the boy's hero worship. He hadn't earned it. All he'd done was try to help a kid like he'd once been feel better about himself. Considering he was a man who avoided entanglements of any kind, it was strange how involved he'd managed to get with both Vala and her son.

He ought to put an end to it. He could, couldn't he?

Yeah, he told himself. Sure. And I suppose you think inviting Vala to spend the night with you under the stars is your first step to disentanglement.

His momentary uneasiness about involvement was erased by a rush of anticipation about what the night might bring, anticipation so intense it filled his mind—and body.

Vala, glancing at Bram, caught his dreamy smile—at nothing—and wondered what he was thinking. Why had he mentioned sleeping under the stars? Now all her thoughts were irrevocably focused on that. She should have said no, but the idea intrigued her.

Or was it the man who intrigued her?

Foolish question. She'd been caught up in something beyond her power to resist ever since he'd walked into that cafe in Apache Junction and looked into her eyes. Though it may have been a mistake to bring Bram back into her life, she was glad she'd ignored that crossed-off name and called him. Never mind that she hadn't expected to feel so drawn to him, he'd made her feel young again, made her feel attractive even in her jeans and long-sleeved shirt trail clothes.

Much as she loved her son, Bram had made her realize there was more to life than being a mother. Not that she'd ever neglect Davis, but she'd been reminded she had a right to a life of her own. A right she just might seize and explore tonight under the stars.

SEVEN

When Vala and Bram arrived at the spot Pauline had sent them to, they found some of the plants she'd mentioned and began clipping off the parts she needed, dropping them into the basket. When it was full, they searched in vain for the other plants she'd described, ones whose roots she'd asked them to dig for her.

"I guess we'll just have to take her what we've got," Vala said.

Bram nodded. "What she wants isn't here. Makes no sense to go on looking when we don't know where else they might grow. Odd that she told us they grew here. As well as she knows the Superstitions, it isn't like Pauline to make such a mistake."

They remounted and soon were threading their way back through a narrow passage between two peaked rock formations. When they came into the open, Vala asked, "Don't you know anything about Pauline other than that she's a medicine woman and a hermit?"

Bram shook his head.

"She acted as though she knew who Davis was talking about when he mentioned Mokesh. That's surely not a common name."

Bram was fairly sure Pauline had Ndee blood, but didn't say so. If Pauline wanted people to know, she could tell them herself. If she didn't, he wasn't going to be the one to say anything.

"I suppose she thinks we're out of our minds to be following that old treasure map," Vala went on. "Oh, not you—I mean Davis and me. Since he's a kid, it boils down to me."

"She wouldn't make that kind of judgment."

"I distinctly heard her say it was crazy to search for gold in the Superstitions."

"You're not searching for gold," he pointed out. "As I keep repeating, treasure doesn't have to be gold."

"Well, no, but in the Superstitions everyone pretty much figures it must be."

"Yeah, the Lost Dutchman Mine and the Apache gold are pegged into the mountain, whether or not they ever were here. Or ever existed."

"You said Apache gold, how come not Ndee."

"That's what the general public calls it. Apache or Ndee, however you think of them, didn't have any interest in what to them wasn't a useful metal, so the chances of them amassing gold is remote. In my opinion, both the legends are little more than fairy tales."

"But you said the Dutchman was a real man."

"He existed, all right. Dutch is what they called Germans in those days and Jacob Walz came from Germany. What I said earlier about him is true, though—he died stone broke. No one has ever proved one way or the other whether he actually did mine for gold or whether the nuggets he once found came from a hidden Spanish cache, one with its own legend."

"So just maybe. . . ." she said softly.

"Don't get fixated on gold," he warned.

"I'm not. But wouldn't it be wonderful if once in awhile a fairy tale came true?"

"They never do." He heard the bitterness in his voice, surprised he still resented his father with such intensity. He thought he'd put that behind him.

Being on this mountain with this woman from his past was stirring up a multitude of emotions, some better left unexplored.

Later, back at the cabin, Vala and Bram enjoyed Pauline's rabbit stew. Davis woke up in time to eat, sitting in a chair padded with a cushion, but acted more sleepy than hungry.

"I don't hurt except a little bit," he told his mother. "Pauline's medicine is working."

"Could the medicine be making him drowsy?" Vala asked her.

"Sometimes does," Pauline said. "No harm to it."

"I'm awake now," Davis insisted. "I been thinking about getting lost and all and I figure maybe it was Coyote playing a trick on me like he does in the stories."

"They *are* just stories," Vala reminded him.

"Yeah, but they mean something. Mokesh said so. He said they wouldn't have gone on telling them for so many years otherwise."

"How did you know Mokesh?" Pauline asked.

Davis explained, ending with, "So, before he died, he gave me an old map and that's why we came here."

"Can I see the map?" Pauline said.

When Bram got it for her from Davis's pack, she held it carefully, examining the drawings on the deerskin by the light of a kerosene lamp.

"Yes, old," she said at last, handing back the map.

"And real," Davis put in. "Mokesh said so."

Pauline nodded. "I met him once when I was very young. How good he found you, boy, before he had to die far away from home without a friend to give his map to."

"Are you Ndee, like him?"

Pauline smiled. "My past is mine. I share it with no one, not even Mokesh's friend. But I tell you one thing true, boy: The map will lead you to your heart's desire."

"My heart's desire?" Davis echoed, sounding surprised. "That's exactly what Mokesh said. I think he meant gold. Is that what you mean?"

Pauline shrugged.

"You're like Mokesh in a way," Davis told her. "He used to say things that he never would explain."

That made her chuckle.

"Maybe we could tell Coyote stories," Davis said. "It's night, so that's the right time."

"Why don't you start?" Bram suggested.

"There's a bunch of them," Davis said. "The first one is how Coyote stole fire, so I'll start with that.

"A long time ago when the animals were people, no one had fire but the Fireflies and they wouldn't give it to anyone."

He went on to tell how Coyote had to outwit them to get a piece of the fire. "But the Fireflies and their friends chased him so he gave the fire to Buzzard. Buzzard got tired after a while and passed it to Swallow, but then the Fireflies made rain medicine and the fire began dying.

"Swallow passed the few coals that were left to Turtle. Turtle put them under his shell where Rain couldn't touch them. Lightning zapped his shell again and again, so that's why Turtle has those marks on his shell today. But he brought fire safely away so everybody could have it."

"Coyote sometimes did good," Pauline said. "But you must remember that Coyote stories have to be told in order."

"That's what Mokesh said. I forget which one's next, though."

Pauline walked to the door and opened it. "Listen, I hear them telling us that's all for tonight."

Vala heard a single coyote's yip-yap, joined by another and then others into a howling chorus.

"Whoa," Davis said, wide-eyed.

"The moon's coming up," Bram put in. "That sets them off."

Bram's penultimate moon, Vala thought.

After Pauline closed the door, without any comment, she began singing in her melodious voice, a plaintive tune in a language Vala didn't recognize. Even though she didn't understand them, the words clearly dwelt on loss and pain and then the gradual return of hope. She'd never heard anything so moving.

"The winter song," Bram murmured. "Ending with the promise of spring." He and Pauline exchanged a long, enigmatic look.

Vala glanced at Davis, waiting for his comment, then noticed his half-closed eyes. He was falling asleep in his padded chair.

Bram rose, reached for Davis, lifting him carefully, and carried him to the cot. Touched by Bram's thoughtfulness, Vala followed and tucked her son in, dropping a kiss on his temple.

"You sang him to sleep," Bram said to Pauline, who neither agreed nor denied it.

"I go to bed early," she told them.

Recognizing a dismissal when she heard one, Vala said good night and headed for the door.

Outside, there was the moon, huge and yellow, part way up the sky, masking the rugged landscape with its silver light. "Penultimate or not, the moon looks full to me," Vala said to Bram.

"Appearances can be deceiving."

She thought of Neal and sighed. He'd seemed so with it, his meanness concealed. She'd taken him for what he projected—a healthy mind in a healthy body type. How could she have been so fooled?

"I'll put the sleeping bags in front of the tent," Bram said.

To keep it convenient for her if she changed her mind? Since she'd made it clear earlier that sleeping under the stars was a maybe, she realized he'd taken her words to heart. What lay concealed under Bram's appearance of thoughtfulness?

She watched him lay the ground sheet on a flat area by the tent opening. Because the tent faced away from Pauline's cabin, this made the tent a barrier between them and the cabin. If they needed a barrier. She knew very well why they might, but she hadn't made up her mind what she should allow the night to bring.

He unrolled his sleeping bag onto the ground cloth; then, holding hers, he glanced at her with one eyebrow raised. Damn the man, he was leaving the choice up to her—in the tent alone or out here with the stars and the moon. And him.

She hesitated, then nodded. Why deny what she wanted? No other man had ever made the world go away when he kissed her. She needed to be with Bram under the stars, not cowering in her tent. If this night together would be all they ever had, why turn down the chance to have this much?

As he rolled out her sleeping bag next to his, her breath caught. Would she regret her decision? No, it was more likely she'd regret it if she didn't take the chance.

Her mind fastened on the gray sweat pants and top she'd been sleeping in and would have to wear tonight. Impossible to picture anything less alluring. Visions of diaphanous nightgowns flashed before her—not that she owned any. Something in red for daring? Or pink for passionate? Or, perhaps a cool blue.

"Found the Big Dipper yet?" Bram said from close beside her.

Lost in her thoughts, she hadn't seen him approach. "What?" she stammered. "Uh, no. Where is it?"

He put his arm around her shoulders and pointed at the sky. When she leaned her head back to look up, it rested against him. Warmth tingled through her, and she gazed up at the seven stars making up the Big Dipper without clearly comprehending what she was looking at.

"Remember which two of them point to the North Star?" he asked.

Leaning against him, breathing in his masculine scent, she couldn't get her mind to focus. "I used to know," she said finally, looking at him instead of at the sky.

He glanced down at her, his eyes turned mysterious by the moon, holding a glint of that silvery light in them. Making a sound very like a growl low in his throat, he pulled her to him and covered her mouth with his. Her lips parted in welcome and the moon, the stars, and the mountain vanished—everything but Bram.

Minutes later, or maybe hours, she couldn't tell, Bram, his arm around her waist, urged her toward the sleeping bags. "Moonlight becomes you," he murmured in her ear, his warm breath sending a shiver of delight through her.

Moonlight altered everything to unreality, she thought, feeling as though she were floating over the ground.

When they reached the sleeping bags, Bram crouched, zipped both of them open, reached for her hand and pulled her down so that they both lay on their backs.

"See the stars," he said softly, raising himself onto one elbow and looking down at her. "I see them in your eyes."

Whether or not the stars were reflected in her eyes, the truth was she was truly starry-eyed, relishing his every word, his every touch.

"All I see is you," she told him, reaching to place her palm against his cheek.

As he lowered his head to kiss her, he murmured something that sounded like "Lighting the fuse."

His kiss, hot and deep, sent tiny fires burning inside her. She wanted more and more, needed to be closer and closer. At the same time, she wished the moment could stretch out and last forever.

Her hands tangled in his hair as she held him to her, their bodies fitted against each other. Her clothes vanished one by one as he caressed her where she longed to be touched. He undressed, too, and they clung together, flesh to flesh.

Urgency thrummed through her as the fires inside her burned brighter and hotter. "Bram," she whispered against his lips, unable to say more than his name.

When at last they joined together, she was quivering with need, the quivers changing to a rhythm that matched his. It was everything. It was . . . it was. . . .

Her mind couldn't hold her thoughts and they exploded into radiating colors as she reached the peak and soared.

Nestled close to Bram afterwards, the second sleeping bag pulled over them, Vala's drowsy content was mixed with wonder. No one had ever made her feel this way before.

"Rockets," Bram murmured.

Vala blinked. "Rockets?"

"I was right about us."

If that made any sense. But, in a way, it did.

After a while, he said, "Sorry I yelled at you about coddling Davis. It can't be easy being a single parent."

"That's okay. You gave me something to think about."

"Let's think about this instead," he said, running a caressing hand over the curve of her hip.

She was more than willing to.

As she came down the second time, the last thing she remembered thinking was: *So it wasn't a one-time phenomenon.*

When she woke the sky was still dark, with the stars shining overhead, but the moon had dropped from sight. Her back was cuddled against Bram and, though he breathed in the deep, even rhythm of sleep, she could feel his arousal pulsing against her, sending an erotic message she couldn't resist.

Half-awake, Bram wasn't sure if he was having a fantastic dream or if Vala was really lying next to him, touching him. Her scent surrounded him, adding to the sensual haze he drifted in as she caressed him.

When she pushed him so he rolled onto his back, he woke up fully, just in time to appreciate every nuance of feeling as she settled herself over him. She was so soft and sweet, her skin like silk under his hands.

It thrilled him that she'd taken control this time, initiating making love. Even as a kid he'd suspected Vala wasn't what she appeared to be on the surface—timid and self-effacing. Maybe that's why he'd been so intrigued by her. He'd wanted to get beneath that facade.

His thoughts melted in the heat of her driving

him up and up until he caught her cry of completion in his mouth and exploded himself.

Lying with her in his arms afterwards, he said, "I knew we'd go up together like rockets if we ever got the fuse properly lit."

"But how do we get it unlit?" she asked.

At the moment, sleepy and temporarily satiated, he couldn't care less.

Bram roused when the coyotes started singing again at dawn. He lay for a moment, breathing in the crisp mountain air, enjoying the feel of Vala's warm body lying next to him. Before he could enjoy it too much, he slid out from under the covering sleeping bag, recovered his strewn clothes and donned them.

Davis wasn't likely to be out exploring early, so there was no reason to be concerned about the boy wondering why his mother and Bram were sleeping together naked. Pauline was a different story. Not that she'd care or tell anyone, but he didn't want her to know what was between him and Vala. This was private, a secret he wanted to share with no one else.

First of all he had to come to terms with it. Sex with women was easy. When it was over, that was the end. Somehow, though, his night with Vala had been more than just sex. It scared the hell out of him.

Vala woke to daylight and saw Bram, fully

dressed, walking away. Without a word. Even though she knew she wouldn't want them to be found lying naked together, it upset her that Bram hadn't so much as offered her a good morning kiss. Or even the words.

Over was over—was that what he meant to convey?

As she fumbled for her clothes, she tried to tell herself she didn't care. There'd been no promises exchanged, after all. Bram had asked her to look at the stars with him. A reluctant smile broke through her hurt—they hadn't seen much of the stars, had they?

Before she headed for the cabin, she zipped up the sleeping bags one at a time, rolled and tied them, leaving no evidence behind. Davis would never understand.

She wasn't any too sure *she* understood. Mostly she felt confused. When she hadn't expected more than the one night they spent in each other's arms, why did she have this aching feeling of loss when she thought there'd be no more? It frightened her.

Once inside the cabin it was clear Davis was feeling like himself again—except for a sore backside. He was torn between his eagerness to go on with the treasure hunt and the realization that it would hurt to ride.

"We'll go along with Pauline," Vala told him. "She says you'll be pretty well healed by tomorrow. So we'll wait until then."

"But Bram told me you already found the bear.

That's the second marker. So only two are left—the snake and the deer. We're almost there."

"They'll still be waiting for us even if we don't hit the trail until tomorrow," she said.

"I have things to teach you, boy," Pauline put in. "You were too sleepy yesterday to understand. Besides, pain doesn't make for a good listener."

"What things?" Davis muttered.

Pauline cast a pointed glance at Bram who was busy stirring oatmeal on the stove. Then she looked at Vala before fastening her gaze on Davis. "Secrets." She hissed the word at him.

His eyes widened. "Really?"

Pauline nodded. "As soon as we get rid of those two. They didn't bring me back the roots I need so they got to hunt for them today. Once they're gone. . . ." She let her words trail off and smiled conspiratorially at Davis.

He smiled back, obviously impatient to be rid of Bram and her, Vala thought, admiring Pauline's deft handling of her son.

But when breakfast was over, cleared away and she and Bram were saddling the horses, Vala wasn't so sure it was a good idea for the two of them to go off alone together. Not that she expected or anticipated a repeat of last night, but for the first time since they'd met again in Apache Junction, she didn't feel at ease with Bram.

Once Val and Bram were mounted, the trail he took only allowed for single horse passage. She followed, not attempting conversation. Pauline had given Bram the directions and her the basket with the digging and clipping gear. All Vala had overheard was Spanish something.

They rode farther than they had yesterday, through rocky defiles and between huge clumps of cacti, until Bram made a sharp right turn between two mesa-like rises. She was surprised to see a clump of palo verde trees. Before they'd only been visible in the ravines and crevices where they'd get the most water, but here they were on the flat.

Bram stopped in the midst of the trees where a tiny spring seeped out and ran into a shallow depression in the rock where it trickled over the edges. It wasn't big enough to be called a pool, but it was water and she gazed at it with avid interest. She hadn't had a decent wash since their second day on the trail.

"Bet I can read your mind," Bram said, dismounting and letting his horse have a drink, tugging him away and tying him to a tree before the gelding bloated himself.

Once Susie Q had her turn at the water and was tethered, Vala said, "We don't get in that pool together."

"You don't get your back washed by yourself," he said, grinning at her.

"My back is the least of my worries. What if someone else is in the vicinity and shows up? One of us needs to stand guard."

"Not everyone knows about Spanish Horse Spring. A chance traveler isn't likely."

"Maybe not, but it's still no."

"That sounds regrettably final. Too bad. Ladies first, then."

"You can't look," she told him before starting to undress.

"Why not?"

Maybe it was unreasonable of her, considering what had happened between them during the night, but she couldn't bring herself to take her clothes off in front of Bram.

"I'm not used to—I mean, I'd be, well, embarrassed," she stammered.

He raised his eyebrows, sighed and turned his back to her. To make sure of as much privacy as she could in case he peeked, she also turned her back to him as she undressed. Naked, she splashed into the shallow pool.

"I forgot to give you Pauline's soap." Bram's voice sounded so close behind her that she whirled.

Soap in hand, he was just stepping into the pool—as naked as she.

EIGHT

"You may not need someone to wash your back, but I do," Bram said, handing her the soap as he turned his back to her.

With him standing in the small, shallow pool next to her, no room was left. "I thought you promised you wouldn't come in until I was done," Vala scolded.

"I didn't promise—you made that assumption," he countered. "My rule is: no promises, no grief. You told me your objections and I appeared to agree, that's all."

Deciding she'd been outmaneuvered, Vala muttered, "Never tangle with a lawyer."

Making the best of it, which wasn't all that difficult to do, she crouched and splashed water up along Bram's back.

"Cold," he complained.

"You're here on sufferance. Don't disturb the backscrubber with trivia," she warned as she soaped his back.

Running her hands over his smooth skin and

feeling the powerful muscles bunched underneath, she found, was *really* disturbing. She'd never realized touching a man could be so erotic. Hurriedly handing the soap back to him, she said, "I'm through. It's all over."

"That's what you think," he said as he turned and splashed water on her, then started soaping her breasts.

"That's not my back," she complained.

"Lady, I wash whatever part's presented," he told her. "Nice parts, by the way."

"You're a wicked man," she said, concealing her amusement as she twisted away from him. She slipped, grabbed at him and they both fell into the shallow water. Warmed by the high-altitude sun, the water was cool but tolerable once they got used to it.

"Not the biggest bathtub in the world," Bram said. "Nor the warmest water. Wait'll I get you in my Jacuzzi."

Vala, taken aback—when did he expect to do that?—started to get up. Bram caught her arm and pulled her down again, this time on top of him. Holding her firmly against him, he kissed her.

All her concern about the possibility of somebody coming and finding them in the pool fled as she melted into the kiss.

Bram had her just where he wanted her—in his arms and naked. Her skin was so very white where the sun didn't reach, white and soft and arousing to caress. Pauline's soap had a faint herbal aroma which mingled pleasantly with Vala's own scent. He wanted her as acutely as he had the night before, with the added edge of having learned how passionate she could be.

He'd had vague dreams when he was young of finding out what she was like under that aloof manner of hers. What he'd finally discovered all these years later was beyond his wildest imaginings.

She was not going to be easy to forget.

Once they were locked together, the world vanished, except for Vala. Rockets didn't begin to describe the way she made him feel. He couldn't get enough of her. He wanted their lovemaking to last and last. Forever.

When he finally peaked and came down, he still didn't want to let her go, but he was afraid she might be getting cold, wet as they both were. With considerable reluctance, he released her.

As they quickly finished washing, she said to him, "I'm perfectly aware you planned this from the very beginning. What does it take to stop you from doing something you've made up your mind to do—a legal document?"

He grinned at her, "Are you complaining?"

She flushed, but looked him in the eye. "Wouldn't you be surprised if I said yes?"

"Under oath?"

"This isn't a courtroom."

"And I couldn't be more grateful. After all, I don't have my tie handy."

"I doubt the judge would be any more lenient if you did have it here." She giggled. "I can just see you naked, but wearing the tie, trying to explain how you seduced a poor innocent maiden."

"Easy. I'd explain you were a princess and so everything that happened was your fault because I was a carefree frog until you kissed me."

It warmed him to watch Vala laugh.

When they were dressed and had remounted the horses, she asked, "Do you think you'll ever go back to being an attorney?"

"I don't rule it out. But not at the moment. Why?"

"Curiosity. I know it must have taken a lot of hard work to get that law degree and pass the bar exam."

"In a way, you drove me to it."

"Me? What on earth do you mean?"

"Once I was a lawyer, the Channings would no longer think I wasn't good enough for their daughter. Something like that."

Taken aback, Vala said, "I can't believe I was that important to you in those days."

"Actually, what I needed to do crystallized for me after our unhappy night of misunderstandings. At the time, it seemed to me law school was the answer."

"So it wasn't me, exactly."

"Don't abdicate responsibility for turning me into a respectable citizen."

"Which you didn't enjoy being?"

"There's such a thing as too respectable. If I hadn't learned that on my own, Sheba, my Siamese cat, would have taught me in her own fashion."

"Back then you always acted as though you knew what you were doing, but I was such a wimpy kid," Vala said. "Not till I divorced Neal did I finally learn to stick up for myself. If I'd learned it *before* I met him, I'd have had enough sense not to marry him."

Bram knew he might be pushing it, but he really wanted to know. "Did you love him?"

She hesitated before answering. "Looking back I'd say no. Infatuated is closer. Neal was a take-charge person and I realize now I simply let him take charge of me, of every facet of our life—until Davis was born. You might say mother love gave me a clear look at the man who was my son's father and I didn't like what I saw. But it took me two more years to get up enough courage to end the marriage."

"You seem to be standing pretty firmly on your own feet now."

"Thank Davis for that. Single moms have to learn to be assertive. Now it's my turn to ask you. Have *you* ever been in love?"

"To use your term—an infatuation or so, nothing lasting."

Vala didn't say anything for a bit; then she

zinged one at him. "Was Lori the Ice Maiden one of them?"

He laughed. "Frozen sherbet's never been one of my favorites."

"You kissed her."

"To win a bet, as you reminded me. I kissed a lot of girls back then."

"But not me."

"Whose fault is that?"

"Maybe the Trickster's."

Vala's tone was light but her words triggered a memory he didn't know he had. The two of them, his father and him, a child, somewhere in the desert on a hot day, driving to see his grandmother.

"Mom misses you," little Bram had said.

"I miss her, too," his dad replied.

"Then how come you don't stay home?"

"The Trickster made me a wanderer and your mother a homebody. I can't stay in one place any more than she can put up with always traveling. It's not easy for either of us."

The child Bram didn't quite understand, even though he knew about the Trickster.

He thought he understood now. They must have loved each other, his mother and father, but had been too different to be able to live together.

What other memories of his father had he repressed into forgetfulness? He'd always blamed his old man for making him live like a kid without a father. For not being there to applaud his successes or help him through his failures. For neglecting him.

Unsettled by the direction his thoughts were taking him, Bram shoved them aside.

"How are your parents?" he asked Vala.

"My dad's still alive. Retired and living in Florida. Mom's been dead three years. I really miss her. She's the only one who supported my divorcing Neal. Dad thought I was giving up security for chaos. Which wasn't far from the truth for a while there. How about your mother?"

"She's living in California with her sister. My father died before I finished law school."

How, he thought, can you miss a man who was never there? A man you resented? Yet he did.

At last they came to the place where Pauline had told them the plants would be growing and found she was right.

As Bram grubbed for the roots, he said, "We did this backward. Should've done the digging first, then the bathing. Of course, we could stop on the way back. . . ."

"In your dreams."

He put down the trowel, made a grab for her and kissed her so thoroughly he managed to get himself aroused. "Guess it'll have to be here, then," he murmured into her ear, only half teasing her.

"You are so bad," she told him, pushing away. "What's Pauline going to think when we come back with only two roots?"

"The truth, probably. I figure she deliberately split our search for the plants into two so she could send us off twice to be alone together."

Vala blinked, then nodded. "I should have real-ized that."

Her unconcern—she didn't care if Pauline knew they'd been making love—puzzled her. Meeting Bram again had turned her world upside down, no doubt of that. Proper Vala had shed inhibitions like leaves from a maple in the fall. And had fun doing it.

Although fun wasn't exactly the right word. Not even close, really. Making love with Bram was like nothing she'd ever experienced. It was so addictive that she kept wanting more and more.

"We can't keep on doing this," she protested when he reached for her again.

"Why not? Tell me you don't want me."

She'd have to lie to do that. About to succumb to the magic of being in his arms, she caught movement from the corner of her eye and froze, staring at a huge black and hairy spider no more than a foot away.

"Tarantula!" she cried, leaping to her feet.

Bram rose more slowly. "They're harmless."

"How can you say that when you know they're poisonous?" Vala kept her gaze fixed on the giant spider, now scurrying away from them toward a clump of cacti.

"If one does happen to bite you, it'd be no worse than a bee sting. Black widows are far more deadly."

She had no doubt Bram, an expert when it came to the Superstitions and what lived here, was right, but it didn't make her any less wary. "Tarantulas *look* dangerous," she muttered.

Poisonous or not, the spider's appearance put an end to even the thought of lovemaking in tarantula territory, at least as far as Vala was concerned. They finished gathering roots and rode back toward Pauline's, singing a song from the time they were teens about flying away.

Vala felt as though she'd done that—flown away from who she was. A line from the song stuck in her mind: ". . . can't go back, never go back . . ."

She wouldn't want to. Bram had set something free she never realized she had. If she could just think about that instead of the trip ending and leaving Arizona. Leaving Bram.

"I remember listening to you play that tune on your guitar in the school parking lot," she said.

"Did you ever wonder if I was playing it for you?"

Vala laughed. "Joker."

"You're right. I was playing it for myself. To get attention. I wouldn't want to see Davis go down that road. The problem is to hold the attention, you have to get wilder and wilder, until you'd rather not remember what all you did."

"He won't be like that!"

Bram shook his head. "I hope not. My mother didn't think I would, either. She was and is a good woman who did her best." He didn't add that what he'd needed was a father, partly because he didn't want to reveal so much, but also because Davis obviously needed one, too.

Unfortunately, Vala could do nothing about the creep who'd fathered Davis and then refused to accept the kid. So what if your son didn't measure up to what you wanted? The important thing was to help him grow in ways he could.

His own father might not have been around much but when he did show up, he never belittled. Any belittling, Bram realized, had been in *his* mind, not in any word or deed of his father's.

As clearly as if he'd heard his father speak, words came into his head. "Doesn't matter what you do as long as you're true to yourself."

He'd heard those words when he was too young to understand and had taken them as a license for wildness. Hadn't remembered them in years. Only now did he realize what his father had been trying to tell him.

"Did anyone ever tell you to be true to yourself?" he asked Vala.

"Not that I—" She paused. "On second thought, maybe that's what my mother meant when she said if I felt in my heart it was right to divorce Neal, then I should go ahead."

"This trip is turning into a confession session," Bram said, thinking he'd already told her far more about himself than he'd ever revealed to anyone. Too damn much.

"That's because it's so easy to talk to you about anything and everything," she told him.

He nodded. She'd hit the nail on the head. She was easy for him to talk to as well. Good thing the trip would soon be over or the devil only knew what she might hear next from him.

Once the trip ended, though, Vala would leave. But they still had tonight to be alone together, he told himself. One more night of holding her in the moonlight, of making love. . . .

"Full moon tonight," he said.

"I hadn't forgotten." He smiled at the promise in her voice.

When they reached the cabin, Pauline checked over the roots they'd brought back, admitted they were the right ones, but added, "Took you long enough to get this lot."

"Yeah," Davis chimed in. "It's way after lunch. We been waiting for you to come back. Pauline needs to tell you guys something about the next marker on the map."

Pauline explained that she figured the snake drawing on the map was meant to be the long squiggly rock formation that used to be called the rattler. "Ain't there no more," she finished. "Broke off a couple years ago into pieces." She looked at Bram. "You ever see it?"

He shook his head.

"Then I best tell you how to find where it was," Pauline said. "What you do is take the trail up to the bear, then look for another trail leading off to your left. . . ."

While Pauline went on giving directions to Bram, Vala fixed her attention on her son. "How's your sore behind?" she asked.

"Real good. Pauline said I could ride at least as far as where the snake used to be. Bram got every sticker out." He lowered his voice. "She told me we need to be careful tomorrow but she thinks we may be okay on account of Mokesh was my friend."

Vala wasn't quite sure what he meant. "Careful because of your accident with the cactus spines?"

His "Nope" sounded so much like Bram's that she smiled.

Davis hesitated before going on, obviously torn between telling all and wanting to hold onto his secret for a while longer. "Maybe we should wait and see," he said finally. "Pauline says a lot of times that's all you can do anyway."

Vala couldn't argue with that.

They had red beans and rice, Creole fashion, for supper with Indian bread. Vala watched with amazement while picky eater Davis—I hate hot stuff, Mom—cleaned his plate.

"Pauline used to live in New Orleans," Davis said. "She let me help her cook supper. Did you know there's voodoo down in Louisiana? They even sell the stuff to make voodoo with in stores. Pauline says most of it's fake, except for once in awhile."

Vala decided to leave well enough alone and keep her mouth shut. Some form of voodoo belief probably did exist in New Orleans. Since Pauline had already assured Davis it was fake—or most of it, anyway—she'd do best not to go into her stock reminder of what was real and what wasn't.

"Pauline and me," Davis added, "we'd rather believe like the Ndee." He looked at Bram. "Tangible's when you can touch something, right? You said gold was tangible. You said the treasure might not be tangible. Pauline told me you were right. I want to know what good is treasure you can't touch?"

"How would Mokesh answer that question?" Bram asked.

Davis thought for a moment before replying. "He'd probably tell me one of his stories, the kind I only sort of could understand. He'd wouldn't ever explain them; all he'd say was, 'Wait, and you'll know.' "

"That's as good an answer as I can give you—wait."

From the look on Davis's face, Vala saw he wasn't satisfied. She decided it was time to divert the talk into another channel.

"Are you all packed for tomorrow?" she asked Davis. At his head shake, she said, "Better get to it now. No point in wasting time in the morning."

"I'm gonna sleep outside in the tent so I can get ready real quick," he told her.

Without intending it, her gaze caught Bram's

and he lifted his shoulders slightly in a resigned shrug. They wouldn't be alone under the full moon tonight.

Which was just as well, she tried to tell herself as she helped Pauline clear the table. She'd already lost far too much of her common sense in Bram's arms.

By the time the three of them left the cabin for their nearby camp, Davis was yawning. He hardly argued when Vala told him it was time to bed down, diving obediently into the tent.

"How about you?" Bram asked her. "Tent or stars?"

"We can't—" she began.

He interrupted. "I know that. But Davis won't be upset if you decide to sleep under the stars."

Bram and she could share that much, she told herself. They could enjoy the night and the stars and the moon together. The romance of it appealed to her.

After giving Davis time to fall asleep, Vala slipped into the tent, undressed, donned her grungy old sweats and emerged with her sleeping bag. She spread it near Bram but not close enough to be able to reach out and touch him.

They lay for a time in their separate sleeping bags, bathed in the moon's silvery light and looking up at the night sky.

"Now I remember which two stars in the Big

Dipper point to the north star," she said finally. "Those two there, by the dipper." She didn't admit the reason she couldn't come up with the answer the night before was because she was lost in his embrace.

The stars were beautiful to look at but they were far off. Bram, beautiful in his own way, lay here almost within reach but, under the circumstances, as far away as the stars. He hadn't offered to kiss her good night. She knew why as well as he did. Neither would ever be satisfied with one kiss, not any more, not when they knew. . . .

Vala sighed and shifted inside her sleeping bag. Frustration was not a companionable emotion.

Bram heard her sigh and knew the reason as surely as if she'd told him. They both would be better off with her inside the tent rather than here where she was barely out of reach. He felt on fire with need for her. Damn, but the woman had gotten under his skin.

If they did make love, chances were good Davis would sleep through it. What if he didn't, though? The kid had enough problems without being confronted with an adult issue like lovemaking. Wouldn't be fair to the boy.

Good kid. He wouldn't do anything to hurt him.

Bram half-smiled. In this case altruism sure as hell paved the way to frustration. He wasn't at all sure he could last the night this close to Vala without touching her.

After a time, a scraping sound tensed him. He sat up to look around and saw Davis dragging his sleeping bag out of the tent toward them.

"Hey, Mom," Davis said to Vala, as he wedged his sleeping bag in between the two of them, "how come you didn't tell me you were gonna sleep out here? You guys get to have all the fun."

NINE

With Davis in his sleeping bag between her and Bram, Vala finally relaxed and slept, the temptation to reach out to Bram gone.

In the morning, they ate a quick breakfast in the cabin. Pauline followed them out and drew Davis aside while they were packing up to leave. Vala couldn't hear what she said, though it evidently surprised Davis because Vala heard his startled "Whoa!" very clearly. He listened some more and then nodded. "Okay, I won't forget," he assured Pauline. About to turn away, he added, "I wish we lived closer to you."

"Things are as they are," Pauline said. "But remember, boy, conditions are always changing for man and beast alike."

She waved to them all, reentered her cabin and closed the door, not waiting for them to ride off.

"Mokesh never said goodbye, either," Davis commented.

They fell into single file with Bram in the lead and Vala bringing up the rear, which made conversation difficult. Once she called ahead to Davis to ask how he was doing.

"Okay," he told her.

Though she tried to keep her mind on today's travel, her thoughts drifted to what was troubling her most. She no longer worried so much about Davis being disappointed if they found no treasure. The trip itself had turned into enough of an adventure to give him something memorable to bring home.

What bothered her was Bram. Or, rather, what had happened between the two of them. No, that wasn't quite right, either. The real problem was how she was going to cope after she was back in New York—without him.

She had no illusions that their coming together was anything more than an interlude to him. How and why had it become more than that to her? Maybe because until now she hadn't had any interest in a man since the divorce.

Shaking her head, she scolded herself—Come on, be honest. You know it's not just the sex. In the first place it wasn't just sex, not with Bram. You made love with him.

Love. The word seemed to hang in the air like a warning beacon.

Bram watched for the subtle landmarks Pauline had told him about, but that didn't take all his attention. His thoughts circled, homing in on what he kept coming back to—Vala. When they started off on this trip, he didn't plan to make love to her. When he realized how badly he wanted to, he'd still tried to control the temptation. Then it became inevitable and he was lost.

He still felt lost. Making love with Vala had set him down on an unfamiliar trail, with no recognizable landmarks. He was traveling blind, uncertain where he was headed. If he'd thought about it at all, he might have believed once he gave way to his driving need for her, he'd be free of it. How was he to know the need would increase with each time they came together?

It scared the hell out of him to even consider there might be more than sex involved, but he'd be lying to himself if he didn't admit his feelings for Vala were one hell of a lot more complicated than that.

He wished the trip was behind him and she was gone. At the same time, he dreaded saying goodbye.

"I see the Needle!" Davis called.

Bram pulled himself out of his reverie. Fine guide he was to miss the tall spire of the outstanding landmark in the Superstitions—Weaver's Needle. There it was, clear as anything, visible between two peaks.

"Didn't Pauline say to keep bearing left?" Davis added.

"You got it." Kid was going to be a helluva guide someday. Good sense of direction, despite his getting lost that once. Knew his way around a horse, too.

Some time later, Bram decided they'd come as close as they were going to get to the place where Pauline had said the snake landmark once was. He called a rest halt.

When Davis slid off his horse, Bram noticed him gingerly rub his rear. Must still hurt some when he rode. They'd make it a short day.

"I wish that old snake hadn't crumbled away," Davis said. "I would've liked to see it."

Bram pointed. "By Pauline's account it hung off that rock over yonder."

A thick stand of greasewood prevented any attempt to get closer to where the landmark snake once was, so Davis tramped around the area looking for a way past the barrier. Bram noticed Vala keeping an eye on her son, but she didn't call out any warnings.

Bram had started to walk over to her when he heard Davis say something. He turned to look.

"Mokesh, Mokesh, Mokesh," Davis chanted in a low tone, over and over.

Bram stared at him, noticing the boy was frozen in position. He changed direction rapidly, heading for Davis. As he came closer, he held, his attention caught by movement on the ground. Snake. The most dangerous kind—rattler.

Not moving, with the familiar snake-sighting chill crawling along his spine, he watched the snake glide in under the greasewood and disappear. Big one.

"Any more?" he called to Davis.

The boy broke from his frozen position and ran to Bram, who put an arm around his shoulders. "One rattlesnake was enough!" Davis told him.

"More than enough," Bram agreed.

"I was watching out 'cause Pauline said I had to be extra careful about snakes today. When he rattled at me, I remembered what you said so I stopped moving. He wasn't coiled so I stayed still and waited and did what Pauline said and sure enough, he didn't try to bite me."

"What happened?" Vala demanded, hurrying up to them. "Are you all right, Davis?"

"He spotted a rattlesnake," Bram said, playing it down.

"He had seven rattles," Davis put in.

Vala glanced around nervously.

"It's okay. He went in the greasewood," Davis assured her.

"I'd still rather get out of here," Vala said.

Bram nodded and they remounted. He wondered why the boy had been chanting Mokesh's name—was that what Pauline had told him to do if he met a rattler? Why would she do that?

Mokesh did have sort of a hissing sound. Ndee words often matched the animal they described. Bram blinked. Where had that thought come from? And why had he suddenly recalled what the word Mokesh meant?

Golden Eyes. Rattlesnake.

The story his father had told him about Mokesh began unraveling in his mind, a story he would have sworn minutes ago that he'd never heard. Another blocked memory. How many of them had he stowed away like that?

Troubled by the realization he'd selectively eliminated another good memory of his father, he passed the rest of the day's trip in a half-daze, paying just enough attention so they didn't get off the right trail. As he'd intended, he called an early halt.

"Doesn't look like we'll find a better place than this for a night camp," he said, noticing that Davis didn't protest. The ride had to be making him hurt.

Once they'd set up and chowed down, Bram asked Davis what Pauline had said about rattlers.

"She told me that's what Mokesh's name meant and if I didn't scare the snake, it'd go away peacefully if I chanted that name over and over. So I did."

"Didn't do any harm," Bram said. "And you remembered what I said about snakes. Smart kid."

"I *was* scared," Davis admitted.

"That's smart, too."

"I'd have screamed," Vala put in.

"Maybe it's a good thing I saw the snake and not you, Mom."

"I'd just as soon neither of us had seen it," she told him.

"Speaking of snakes," Bram said, "when it gets dark it's my turn to tell a story." Very deliberately, he added, "It's one my father told me when I was a kid. He wasn't around much but when he was, we did things together."

As he spoke, Bram felt something give way within him. Was it because he'd never before said anything good about his father?

"My father doesn't do much with me," Davis said matter-of-factly. " 'Cause I'm a poor athlete."

Bram wasn't going to let it rest at that. "You mean in team sports."

"Yeah."

"I noticed you have a good sense of balance and I mentioned to your mother that I think you'd do well on skis. That's a sport you can do alone."

Davis stared at him. "Skiing? You really think I'd do okay?"

"Hey, good balance is half the battle."

Davis's pleased expression rewarded him.

As the evening slipped into night, Vala began posing riddles. Davis knew most of them, but she caught Bram on several. He dredged a few up from his younger years and finally caught her on one. They were laughing together when he noticed Davis's speculative gaze shifting from one to the other of them and wondered why. It made him uneasy.

"The snakes must be asleep by now," Bram said abruptly. "Time for my father's tale."

He told them about the wounded stranger the Ndee welcomed into their camp and how the old medicine man, Mokesh, meaning Yellow Eyes, cured him.

"When enemy soldiers came for the stranger and demanded him, the Ndee refused to give up the man, even though warned that, as a result, a great enemy force would soon come through the mountain pass and kill every man, woman and child of the Ndee.

"Mokesh listened to the Great Spirit and understood what he must do to save his people. He would stand guard in the narrow pass and stop the enemy warriors.

"The Ndee didn't see how he could stop more than one man, but when he looked at them with his yellow eyes, they believed him. And so, instead of fleeing, they remained in their camp, waiting and watching."

Bram told how the enemy warriors laughed at the old man facing them with nothing more than a medicine rattle and a stick with two curved points at the tip.

"But when they charged at Mokesh, the warriors fell back screaming in pain. Before their eyes he changed into a gigantic spirit snake with huge yellow eyes and two enormous fangs, a snake whose tail bore rattles. Many warriors died from the poisonous bite of Mokesh and the rest ran off, afraid of the Guardian of the Ndee."

"Mokesh turned into a rattlesnake!" Davis exclaimed. "That's why he had yellow eyes to begin with, 'cause rattlers do. And that's why Mokesh means rattler, too."

Bram nodded.

"I bet old Mokesh knew that story. I wonder why he never told it to me?"

"Maybe he didn't live long enough," Vala suggested. "He must have known many, many stories. More than he had time to tell you."

Davis nodded. "Yeah, I guess. He told me once he chose stories I needed to hear. Maybe he even knew I'd come to the Superstitions with his map and meet Bram and hear the Mokesh story."

"Who knows?" Bram said, expecting Vala to chime in with a reminder about reality.

She didn't.

"Now I know why Pauline told me to chant Mokesh's name if I met a rattler," Davis said. "Mokesh is really a Ndee spirit." He looked at Bram. "How come your father knew that story?"

Bram shrugged.

Davis opened his mouth, glanced at his mother, and closed it again. Bram hadn't seen her expression but he could visualize the quit-asking-personal-questions frown she'd given her son.

Bram wasn't sure why he hadn't admitted the truth. Davis, he knew, would be pleased. And Vala? He'd been with her long enough to believe she wouldn't care one way or the other. So why hold back? Damned if he knew.

"We all gonna sleep under the stars again tonight?" Davis asked. As soon as he said the words, he looked stricken. "Oh, maybe I won't," he added.

"I'll share the tent with you," Vala said.

Davis blinked and cast a glance at Bram.

"Don't you want me to?" Vala asked her son.

"Uh, I guess so."

Bram wondered what the devil was bugging the kid.

He hadn't behaved like this last night. Did it have anything to do with what Pauline had said to him this morning?

"I'm hitting the sack," Davis told them and scurried off to the tent.

"What's gotten into him?" Vala asked.

"Beats me. It's just as well. Having you within arm's reach with Davis between us is a waste of moonlight."

"I don't think the moon cares about your opinion. It'll shine anyway. But I agree that it's just as well you're sleeping by yourself in the moonlight."

Bram was silent for a bit. "We'll spot the last marker tomorrow," he said finally. "The place marked with the X isn't far from that point. With luck our journey will be over."

"And the treasure found."

"You're still expecting something tangible?"

Vala sighed. "I don't know what to expect. Davis needs something, some closure to this treasure hunt."

Bram pushed back the words he wanted to say. *What about us? We need closure as much as he does.*

"I guess I'll turn in." Vala started to stand up.

He caught her arm and pulled her back down and into his arms. A good night kiss wasn't all he wanted but he intended to stop there.

The kiss lasted longer than he meant it to. He'd thought he was long past the stage when a kiss could turn his world upside down. Wrong. It took a lot of willpower to end the embrace and let her go.

Vala all but fled to the tent. If she'd stayed any longer in Bram's arms she didn't know what might have happened. She changed into her sweats and slid into the sleeping bag.

"Mom?" Davis's voice was sleepy.

"Yes, honey?"

"I saw you and Bram kissing. That means you like each other?"

"You could say that, yes. Why?"

"I just wondered. I like him, too. He's way cool."

Vala wasn't going to argue about that. "Is there anything else you want to tell me?" she asked, remembering her son's odd behavior earlier.

"Uh, not right now, okay?"

After they exchanged good nights, she lay awake listening to the rhythm of Davis's breathing change into the sleep mode. Then she heard a single coyote call. No answer came. Could it be searching for a mate? How sad if the coyote never found one.

When she realized she was on the verge of tears, she shook her head, telling herself she was being ridiculous. More than likely that lone coyote was the Trickster, looking for trouble.

And just when had she dropped out of reality

and begun to believe in Apache—no, Ndee—legends? Would she never get that straight?

Still, believe or not, on those days when everything went wrong for no particular reason, it was almost as though there were a trickster out there somewhere playing games.

Strange what thoughts came into your head when you camped out in the wilderness. Probably because you had time to think rather than being constantly busy.

Tomorrow they'd reach the end of their journey. After that was the trip back. Then the return flight to New York.

This time she couldn't stop the tears.

In the morning, Bram had barely crawled out of his sleeping bag before Davis, fully dressed, bounced from the tent. He gazed up at the sky lightening toward dawn and said, "We're gonna find the treasure today."

"How can you tell?" Bram asked.

"We're almost there, aren't we?"

Bram nodded. "But, at the moment, we're here, not there." He examined the sky and frowned. Though not completely overcast, he didn't like the look of what clouds there were.

"Sometimes you sound like Pauline," Davis complained.

"Thank you for the compliment. She's a wise woman."

Davis looked momentarily confused and was silent for a bit. Finally he said, "I saw you and my mom kiss last night, so I asked her if she liked you and she said she did. You must like her, too. Otherwise you wouldn't kiss her."

"Good logic, kid. If I didn't like her I wouldn't want to kiss her."

Like wasn't the right word, but would have to do since he didn't have a substitute.

"I told my mom I liked you, too," Davis went on.

Bram grinned at him. "I never met a nine-year-old boy I liked better than you."

Davis grinned back at him.

"So now can we conclude the mutual admiration society and start making breakfast?" Bram asked.

Davis chattered away about the treasure as he helped. "If it's gold, I'm gonna buy Mom a house. Houses are bigger than apartments and you can have lots of pets if you want and a big yard."

"And if it isn't gold, then what?"

"I guess that depends on what else it is."

No disputing that logic. "Do you like living in New York?" Bram asked.

"It's okay. I never lived anywhere else. I think the desert's kind of neat, though." Vala was emerging from the tent and, spotting her, Davis called, "Do you like the desert, Mom?"

"I'd forgotten how wonderful it was," she said.

Davis exchanged a look with Bram. "Your mother has this tendency to not quite answer a question," Bram told him. "The older you get, the more you'll discover most girls and women do the same thing. It's good you're getting an education this early. You'll need it."

"Mostly you can understand if you think about it," Davis said.

"I agree. It's one of those things men just have to accept."

"I hope you two are through talking about me as though I wasn't even on the same planet," Vala put in. "If we didn't have to get an early start, I'd list the problems women have with men."

"So, okay, you do like the desert then, Mom?" Davis persisted.

"Yes. How's that for a right-to-the-point answer? Why do you ask, anyway?"

"I just wondered."

After breakfast, the three of them acted as a team in cleaning up, repacking and saddling the horses. Watching as Vala pitched in and did her share, Bram decided it wouldn't take much to make her a real outdoorswoman.

"So we're off to find the deer landmark," Vala said once they were mounted.

"The trail seems pretty clear," Bram commented, glancing up at the sky again. "Should be an easy trip if the rain holds off."

Vala looked up and frowned. "Those don't look like storm clouds."

"They're not. Rain clouds."

"No thunder and lightning?" Davis sounded disappointed.

"Can't have everything."

"Are we gonna have to stop and camp early if it rains a lot?" Davis asked.

"Let's hope not," Bram said. "A little rain won't melt us. Neither will a lot, but a downpour makes for heavy going. I don't think we'll get that kind of rain today."

"You know," Davis said, "I just remembered that Mokesh's eyes weren't all brown. His left eye had two chunks of sort of a golden-yellow in the brown. So he was named right."

"We'll hope his map is right, too," Bram said.

Then the trail narrowed and they had to go single file again.

After finding the deer marker without much difficulty, they took a rest break. Before they started up again, Bram discovered the packhorse was definitely going lame. He checked all four hooves but found nothing to account for the problem. The supplies were fewer than when they started, so the horse was carrying an increasingly lighter load. In any case, Bram never overloaded the horses he used.

"This'll slow us down," he said.

As they remounted, a slow drizzle began which soon made the trail difficult for the horses. The rain made the humans equally miserable.

"Maybe the spirits don't want us to get there," Davis said.

"Reality check," Vala put in. "Legends that are

a part of another culture aren't to be taken as absolutely true."

"Aw, Mom, it's fun to imagine they might be watching us right now."

Bram kept his mouth shut. No gain in jumping in when they both had made points he could live with. After a time, he spotted what looked like a good place to camp and made a decision.

"We'll stop, set up the tent and the extension and get in out of this rain," he said. "It'll also give the packhorse a chance to rest his leg."

Davis looked unhappy but he didn't protest.

When the necessary chores were taken care of, including setting up the tent and attaching the extension, the three of them ducked inside and dried off as best they could.

"Bummer," Davis said gloomily. "We're so close to the treasure."

Vala put her arm around him and he leaned against her for a few minutes before pulling away. "Hey," he said, "I just remembered it's Mom's turn to tell a story."

"My turn? How come?" Vala protested.

" 'Cause I told one about Coyote at Pauline's and after we saw the rattler Bram told about Mokesh being the Guardian of the Ndee. So you're next."

"But I don't know any Native American stories," she said.

"Didn't Grandpa or Grandma ever tell you any stories when you were little?" Davis asked.

Vala shook her head. "My father read stories to me and so did my mother."

"I don't mean stories out of books. I guess you'll just have to make up one, then."

"I'm not good at making up stories. It'd have to be a real one. Wait, something's coming to me my grandmother once told me. It's about when she was a little girl. Will that do?"

"Sure!"

"It's sort of sad."

"That's okay, 'cause this is sort of a sad day."

Bram thought Davis was more right than he knew. The day *was* sad. Not because of the rain or the lame horse or the fact they'd had to stop short of their goal. Time would take care of those things.

He felt sad because he'd faced the fact that this trip wasn't going to last forever. All too soon they'd be back in Phoenix. Then only he would be left in Phoenix. Vala and Davis would be gone.

He supposed he'd forget them eventually, as the memories faded and disappeared. But that might well be a long and painful process, one he didn't care to contemplate. His own fault for letting it happen, for identifying with the kid because of his own childhood. As for Vala. . . .

Bram sighed. There was no accounting for Vala.

TEN

Inside the tent, Vala eased into a more comfortable sitting position on her sleeping bag. The gear in the extension smelled not unpleasantly of wet leather and horse, while outside the rain drizzled down.

She let her gaze drift from Davis to Bram, and back. The coziness of them being close together like this gave her a warm feeling.

"My mother's mother's name was Ella," she began her story. "Davis, she'd be your great-grandmother. When she was a little girl of six, her parents took her with them on a trip from Iowa where they lived to visit her mother's parents in Southern California."

"My great-great-grandparents?" Davis asked.

Vala nodded. "In the olden days, Ella said, Los Angeles wasn't the huge metropolis it is now. The parks had carousels and ponds with boats and swans. Eastlake Park was near where Ella was visiting and every day her grandfather would walk down the hill with her to that park. He'd give her some change and tell her she could ride the merry-go-round until the money ran out. Of course, if she caught the gold ring, she'd get a free ride.

"Ella loved riding the carousel horses and every time she went by the ring dispenser, she grabbed one. But it was never the gold one. As she went round, she could see her grandfather sitting on a bench attached to a picnic table where he was playing cribbage with a friend. She knew it was cribbage because her parents played the game at home. Every once in awhile he'd look at her and wave."

Vala went on to tell how Ella finally found out her grandfather's friend had to bring the cards and cribbage board to the park because her grandmother thought cards were the devil's playthings and didn't allow them in the house. Ella didn't know if that was true—her mother said it wasn't—but she was solidly on her grandfather's side, so she never mentioned what he did at the park while she rode the merry-go-round.

"One day, the magic happened—Ella reached out while going around and caught the gold ring. She was so excited she failed to keep a good grip and she dropped it. An older boy jumped off his horse, grabbed the gold ring and wouldn't give it back. When the ride ended, Ella told the man who took care of the carousel, but he said whoever had the gold ring in his hand won the free ride."

"That was mean," Davis said. "What'd she do?"

"Ella went crying to her grandfather. He agreed it was unfair but pointed out there was nothing to be done about it. Even the mean boy had vanished by now. He comforted her until she stopped crying.

"By the time they got home, Ella had somehow twisted the unfair rule around to apply to her grandmother not letting her grandfather play cards in his own house. If she'd kept her mouth shut, everything would have been all right, but Ella, still upset about the gold ring, confronted her grandmother, asking why she was so mean to Grandfather.

"So then it all came out. Grandmother labeled Grandfather a backsliding sinner and lectured Ella's parents about their wayward child. They got upset and left California sooner than they'd planned. On the way home to Iowa, they told Ella she had too big a mouth and let this be a lesson. Before they visited again, Grandfather died and Ella always wondered if it wasn't somehow her fault."

"Whoa, that's way sad," Davis said.

"Is there a moral?" Bram asked.

"Yeah," Davis replied. "Don't drop the gold ring."

"Life isn't always fair," Vala put in.

"I can go along with both of those," Bram told them, "but I have a different one. Don't let something that upset you in the past color your whole life."

Vala stared at him. "That's just what happened to my Grandmother Ella. She always blamed herself when anything went wrong. I never thought about it before."

"If she hadn't dropped the gold ring, she'd've been all right," Davis insisted. "Let's not talk about any more sad things. We could tell jokes. Me first."

Though Vala laughed in the right places and even told a few jokes of her own, her mind kept going back to her Grandmother Ella. Finally she realized why. Ever since she'd divorced Neal, she'd shied away from any kind of a meaningful relationship with a man. In effect, she'd done what Ella had done. After she "lost" her wedding ring by getting divorced, she'd been afraid to take another chance.

Why? It wasn't all her fault that the marriage had failed. Neal was as much to blame as she was. Yet he hadn't let it bother him. Look at him with another wife and another son already.

It wouldn't have helped to keep the damn ring, along with the marriage. She and Neal had been miserable together. They were better off apart.

So now what did it mean that she'd plunged headlong into involvement with another man? A hopeless involvement. Was it due to a twist in her defense mechanism? Bram was safe to fall for because there wasn't a chance for anything permanent between them? No wedding ring, no failure?

"Mom," Davis said, nudging her, "it's your turn to tell a joke."

"I think you'd better skip me this time," she said. "I'm all joked out."

* * *

As the day slipped into an early evening and the rain turned into a heavy mist, it became clear there'd be no sleeping under the stars tonight. Since their gear took up most of the extension, obviously they'd be bedding down in the tent's close quarters.

Vala tried to figure out a way to keep Davis between Bram and her but the configuration of the tent lent itself best to an arrangement whereby Davis, being shorter, slept behind their heads at the rear of the tent.

"I'll turn the sleeping bags around," Bram said, "so Davis will be at our feet instead. We're less likely to wake each other up that way."

"Yeah," Davis agreed. "Sometimes Mom snores a little."

"I do not!" Vala said.

"Want me to let you know in the morning?" Bram asked her, chuckling.

She flushed, realizing he probably already knew whether she did or not. Tonight, she decided, was not going to be peaceful.

When they were settled into their sleeping bags, Davis said, "This is fun."

For you, maybe, she thought, lying rigid, unable to relax with Bram practically nestled against her.

"It's sort of like summer camp," Davis went on, "but more like we're a family camping in our tent."

His words fell painfully onto Vala's heart.

Bram tried to think of some quip to toss into the silence that stretched out after Davis's last remark, but he couldn't come up with a thing.

He knew what the kid meant. Often during one of his guide trips, the people who'd hired him, sometimes strangers to one another, developed a sense of camaraderie born of shared hardships on the trail. He'd always stayed aloof, friendly without making anyone a comrade.

This time he'd screwed up. For one thing, he rarely had as few as two people to guide. But what had really got to him was who the two people were. Vala and Davis. He'd gotten to know them so well it seemed incredible that they'd soon be more than half a continent away from him.

His thoughts drifted to the story Vala had told about her grandmother. He'd picked up on what he saw as the moral to be learned from the tale because he'd been guilty of using his version of the past to color his world. What if, as he'd been slowly coming to realize, his version was skewed?

His father hadn't really neglected him, even if he wasn't around much of the time. When they'd been together, which seemed to be more often than Bram had once believed, his father had done the best he could to teach his son what he felt was important, to offer as much of his heritage as a kid could understand.

Bram sighed, belatedly noting his sigh was intermingling with Vala's. "Can't sleep?" he asked softly.

"Too many ghosts of the past hovering," she said. "I guess I shouldn't have told Ella's story."

If he moved even slightly, they'd be touching.

Two sleeping bags made a lot of padding between them, but he decided not to risk it anyway.

"I know what you mean," he admitted. "Plus this intimate sleeping arrangement where we can't be intimate."

"That, too."

"Davis asleep?"

"His breathing sounds as though he is," she said.

"When we started on this trip," Bram said slowly, feeling his way along, "I didn't expect what happened to us to happen, if that makes sense."

"Neither did I. It was the farthest thing from my mind. For the first two days I was mad at you most of the time."

"Come to think of it, I was damned annoyed with you, telling me you could ride when you'd never been on a horse. But I have to admit you proved to be a quick learner."

"And I acquired the sore muscles to prove it."

"You might be a liar, Vala, but you proved you're a good sport."

"A lie told to help someone else doesn't count."

"As Davis would say—whoa. Some definition."

"Consider yourself warned."

All the warning signs had been there, Bram realized—the girl from his past, the old attraction reviving with the added spice of her now being an adult, the rising desire. He'd noted and ignored each and every one, plunging on like a desperately thirsty man heading for water.

Served him right if he drowned.

"Davis saw us kiss last night," he said.

"I know. He figures we must like each other."

"Don't we?"

"I refuse to answer on the grounds it might incriminate me."

"Coward."

"Better safe than sorry."

"Is it?"

She didn't answer.

What did he want from her other than what he knew they had? He wasn't sure. This yearning he felt was something beyond his experience.

"Falling asleep?" she asked.

"Not yet."

"Tell me something about you that I don't know," she said.

She already knew too much about him. He searched for something innocuous to tell her and Sheba popped into his mind.

"My cat," he began. "I didn't pick Sheba out; she just happened to me. Showed up as a half-grown kitten yowling on my front doorstep a little over a year ago. No one in the neighborhood claimed her. The gal next door thought the kitten might have belonged to the people across the street who'd moved out a couple days before.

"Sheba was hungry and lonesome, equal parts of each. I'd never been around Siamese cats, didn't realize they talked to you. Or grew on you. Or were completely zany felines. After a couple of days we bonded and now we're stuck with each other."

"What becomes of Sheba when you're off guiding?"

"My friend Nick from across town likes cats, so he takes care of her when I'm away."

"You said she had kittens."

"Sheba got it into her head that's what she wanted. You ever try to change a Siamese cat's mind? The people down the block had a Siamese male so we arranged a rendezvous. She hated him on sight but, after we left them alone together in my utility room overnight, Sheba changed her mind.

"The eventual result was five kittens. Believe me, after they're old enough to leave, Sheba gets spayed."

"Why? Did she get sick?"

He shook his head. "What she did was refuse to give birth to a single one of them unless I sat on the floor beside the box I'd fixed and talked to her while she had them. Hell, I was as nervous as a new father."

Vala chuckled. "So she didn't have any trouble."

"No, but I did. The third kitten she delivered was a lot smaller than the first two. Instead of washing it off like she'd done with the others, Sheba nosed it aside, delivered the fourth and proceeded to clean it up. Despite the fact I kept shoving the tiny one in her face, she refused to give it a single lick. Finally, when she'd cleaned the fifth, she decided I wasn't going to give up so she might as well accept the runt of the litter."

"Is it doing all right?"

"He. Feisty little thing despite his size and original nonacceptance. Sheba treats him now just like she does the others. I did some research and found animals often push the runt of a litter aside and let it die. A runt is likely to have defects and somehow they sense that."

"Sounds cold-blooded, but I suppose in the wild it'd be logical to give the bigger, healthier ones a better chance."

"Something like that." It gave him a pang when it came to him that Davis's father had behaved in just such a way to his own son. He hoped the thought wouldn't occur to Vala. Davis was definitely not a misfit to be cast aside.

Vala was surprised by a yawn. She hadn't realized she was getting tired. "Good night," she murmured.

"Good night, sweet princess," he told her. "I promise you won't hear a single ribbet from me all night."

She smiled at the frog reference, but refused to dwell on what she knew had inspired it. She'd never get to sleep if she did.

I wonder if he realizes he completely melted my heart with that story about Sheba, she asked herself. *How many men would be so caring?* None she knew well. Not her father and certainly not Neal.

How wonderful it would be if she could fall asleep in Bram's arms. He was near enough that she could, very faintly, smell his essence. Breathing it in, she closed her eyes and tried to imagine herself snuggled inside the sleeping bag with him, her head on his shoulder while he held her against him. . . .

A cry woke Vala. It took her a moment to realize where she was and that what she'd heard was Davis. As she struggled to sit up, Bram's flashlight clicked on, its beam centered on her son who was muttering unintelligibly as he thrashed around in his sleeping bag.

Before she'd extricated herself from her own bag, Bram reached Davis and gathered him into his arms, sleeping bag and all. Half in and half out of her sleeping bag, she sat up and watched them.

"Hush," he murmured. "Everything's all right. Bram's here. Don't fight me. I won't let anything hurt you."

As Bram continued to soothe the boy, gradually Davis stopped struggling and lay quiet again.

"The pediatrician calls it a night terror," Vala said as Bram eased boy and sleeping bag back down. "Davis has a bout every once in awhile. It's something like a nightmare except the child doesn't wake up. The doctor said it can be related to sleepwalking but, thank heaven, Davis has never done that."

Belatedly she noticed that Bram wore a T-shirt

and his undershorts to sleep in. A lot more revealing than her sweats.

"Will he have another bout tonight?" Bram asked.

She had to stop staring at him. "No, he never seems to do that. He should be okay till morning. Thanks for coping."

Bram, now focusing the beam of the flashlight up toward the tent roof, looked at her without speaking.

"What's the matter?" she asked, disturbed by his intent gaze.

"Never thought I'd find a gray sweatshirt sexy," he muttered. "Better douse the damn light and crawl into my straitjacket before it's too late." He clicked it off.

Her eyes dazzled by the light, Vala found the darkness in the tent absolute. The same thing must have happened to Bram because he cursed. Then he stepped on her foot. Even though her foot was protected by her sleeping bag, it still hurt and she tried to jerk her foot away.

This must have tipped him off balance because, the next thing she knew, Bram was sprawled over on her so that she was no longer sitting, instead she was lying half out of her sleeping bag. Without thinking what she was doing, she put her arms around him.

With a groan, he gathered her to him, settling his mouth over hers in a kiss that demanded even as it offered. His hands slid under the sweatshirt and caressed her bare skin, setting her on fire.

She knew there was a reason she must stop, must stop him, stop them both—but the reason seemed just out of reach. The reality was Bram and the urgent desire sizzling between them, luring her on.

Bram was starting to ease Vala out of her sleeping bag, when enough sanity returned so he remembered Davis. He stopped, letting her go.

He heard Vala release a long sighing breath. She must know why he'd halted the lovemaking, but he figured she couldn't possibly feel as frustrated as he did. Damn, but he wanted this woman. Not at the risk of Davis waking, though. The poor kid—as if having a night terror wasn't bad enough. He didn't need to be confronted with adult reality besides.

As he crawled into his sleeping bag, Bram shook his head. Doing the right thing could be damn uncomfortable.

In the morning, Bram woke to Davis's voice.

". . . dream about Mokesh," the kid was saying.

"A bad dream?" Vala asked. Her question wasn't surprising, considering the night terror.

Davis hesitated, finally saying, "Sort of."

Bram eased himself from his sleeping bag until he could sit up. Both Davis and Vala were still snugged up in theirs.

"Hi, Bram," Davis said. "I was telling Mom

about my dream." He frowned. "I think you were in it somewhere. Anyway, I dreamed I found the treasure and it *was* gold. Lots and lots of gold nuggets. I picked up some to look at and all of a sudden Mokesh was standing there.

" 'No,' he told me, 'that's not what you need.' I looked at the gold nuggets to be sure they were still there and when I looked back at Mokesh he wasn't an old man anymore." Davis's breath caught. "He'd turned into this great big really scary rattlesnake.

"He rattled his tail loud, like he was mad. I tried to get away from him and dropped all the nuggets. Mokesh hissed at them and they melted away and were gone.

"I got really scared then. I think that's when you were there, Bram. It's kind of fuzzy. But anyway, the snake disappeared and I don't remember any more."

"I'd say that qualifies as a bad dream," Bram told him.

"Finding the treasure was a good part, though."

"If we don't get started," Vala put in, "we won't find anything. Who's getting up first?"

Bram slid the rest of the way out of his sleeping bag and stood up, hunching over in the low tent. He opened the flap and assessed the day.

"Cool, some clouds, no rain," he reported.

"It looks like Bram is first up," Vala said.

"Me second," Davis insisted. "Mom, you got to close your eyes while Bram and me get dressed."

It amused Bram that she did close her eyes to humor the boy.

He and Davis were getting breakfast by the time Vala emerged from the tent.

Later, as they dragged the saddles from the extension and pulled down the tent, Davis said, "I bet it really will be gold. My dream was an omen."

"Your dream was not an omen." Vala's voice was unusually sharp. "Dreams reflect what's going on inside our minds; they don't predict the future."

Davis gave her a sulky look.

"Even if you wanted to think of your dream as an omen," Bram pointed out, "didn't Mokesh himself tell you the gold wasn't the treasure? What about that part?"

Scowling at Bram, Davis said, "You and Mom are spoiling everything."

"Fantasies stop being fun when people begin to believe them," Vala warned.

Bram winced inwardly. He was beginning to be tempted to believe in his own fantasy, which had nothing to do with finding gold. Her warning came as a timely reminder not to lose his head.

By the time they mounted up and left the camp, Davis had lost his sullen expression, but he wasn't talking. Neither was Vala. What had happened to the camaraderie of the night before? The only bright spot was that the packhorse seemed less lame.

Some time later, Vala, obviously attempting to lighten everyone's mood, began singing about them being off to see the Wizard of Oz. Bram, brooding some himself by then, thought she'd chosen the perfect tune. He'd seen dozens of treasure maps and he'd never yet seen an authentic one.

Mokesh's map would prove to be as fake as the "wonderful wizard" Dorothy and her friends were off to see.

He was willing to bet that no gold, no silver, no jewels waited for them at the spot marked X. In fact, he thought they'd find nothing at all.

ELEVEN

The trail they followed was the steepest yet, the horses laboring uphill for what seemed an endless time. When they finally came out onto a more or less level area, Bram called a halt and they dismounted.

"Let's see that map again," he said to Davis.

Davis extracted the map from a saddlebag, handed it to him and then stood close to peer at it with him. Vala joined them to stare down at the deerskin.

"This is it," Bram declared after a few minutes' study. "The end of the road."

"You mean the treasure is here?" Davis asked, looking around eagerly.

"As far as I can tell." Bram rolled the map back up and handed it to Davis. "Better put this away before we go haring off to search."

Davis made the run to the saddlebag and back in record time.

"Listen up," Bram announced. "No splitting the search party. We three stick together at all times. Is that clear?"

No one objected.

"We'll start to the far left and search the outer areas in a clockwise rotation," he went on. "Don't any of you figure it's going to be easy to find whatever it is we're searching for. Look sharp."

They'd covered half the outer rim when Davis cried, "My foot hit something."

Bram knelt and dug around a metallic chunk with a small collapsible spade from his gear. Vala held her breath as he eased the object free. What was it?

"I'd say this is the broken-off end of a pickax," Bram announced. "Whether or not there's any gold here, somebody had a fling at digging for it."

Judging from the broken point of the pickax, which resembled some old relic, Vala figured the digger had been here a long time ago. She held out her hand and Bram gave her the piece of metal.

Vala intended to save it—just in case. If nothing else turned up, at least Davis would have a souvenir from the trip.

As they went on, they came to a mound of broken rocks. Glancing up, Vala saw the rocks had come from a shattered spire thrusting high above.

She noticed Bram follow her gaze. "Remember, the Superstitions are of volcanic origin," he said. "There are a couple of great cones down at the west end."

Davis made a sweeping gesture, "You mean a volcano made all this?"

Bram nodded. "A *long* time ago."

"Everything interesting happened before I was born," Davis complained. "Like the dinosaurs and all."

"Then I guess you'll just have to find something interesting to do with your life," Vala told her son.

"Like find the treasure," Davis said.

As they continued around the rim, Davis spotted what looked like it might be the opening to a mine, but it turned out to be no more than a shallow hole in the rock.

They finished the circle without finding anything else.

"With our next clockwise sweep," Bram said, "try hard to spot anything unusual."

He was saying this, Vala figured, because once they finished making the second, inner circle, there was no other place to search. Find it this time or it isn't here.

She hadn't allowed herself to believe there'd be gold at the end of the journey, but she'd hoped all along to be proved wrong. Turning the broken piece of metal over in her hands, she resigned herself to this fragment being all they'd discover.

Near the center of the area rose a rounded dome-like formation with smaller rocks scattered around it and some larger ones on top. On the far side, a large pile of rocks suggested something had broken off at one time or another and slid down here in pieces.

A different colored rock caught Vala's eye, whitish instead of the red-brown prevailing color. Curious, she reached into the pile to try to pull it loose to examine it but found what she'd grasped was the small end of a large rock. Determined not to be thwarted, she gave a hard yank.

Instead of the rock pulling free, the entire pile shifted and she jumped back to avoid the tumbling rocks. The noise brought Davis and Bram from the other side of the formation.

"I saw this rock I wanted to look at—" she began to explain before Davis cut her off.

"Look!" he cried, pointing. "There's a hole."

Vala eyed the long gap the falling rocks had revealed. Just a crevice—or something more?

It took the three of them almost an hour to shift enough of the rocks so Bram could shine his flashlight into the opening. Vala watched Davis fidget when Bram continued to look inside, not moving or speaking.

"What's in there?" Davis finally demanded.

Bram pulled back and handed Davis the flashlight. "See for yourself."

Davis inched closer and shone the light inside the cavity. After a moment or two, he pulled his head out, his mouth drooping in disappointment. "Just some old pictures somebody drew on the rock in there."

Vala took the flashlight from him to discover what he was talking about. She was gazing in fascination at the strange drawings inside when she heard Bram speak.

"Okay, Davis, I want you to use that smart brain of yours. What do those drawings remind you of?"

"Uh—nothing much. Sort of like a little kid's drawing."

"You're not thinking. Where have you seen drawings like that lately?"

Vala pulled her head out in time to see her son's face light up. "On the map!" he cried. "On Mokesh's map."

She nodded. They were very similar.

"So what does that mean?" Bram persisted.

Looking at him, Vala realized there was something different about Bram, a sort of brightness in his face she hadn't noticed before.

"Mokesh said the map was made before his time," Davis said slowly. "So whoever made it lived way long ago. His Ndee ancestors, maybe." He reached up and tugged at his ear. "So those drawings in there have to be real old, too, don't they?"

Bram nodded. "They're called pictographs. Native Americans drew them in many places in this country. But no one is sure how old the drawings are. Sometimes these same symbols are found carved in rocks."

"Petroglyphs," Vala said, remembering a display she'd seen in a New York museum. She realized now that they'd found something of incredible value in these rock drawings.

"Right," Bram said. "If Mokesh were alive, he'd tell us the Ndee found those pictographs when they settled around here a long time ago. He'd say people they call the Old Ones drew them."

"Who were the Old Ones?" Davis asked. "Mokesh told me they were here before the Ndee but he didn't explain. Except to say they were still here."

"He meant their spirits remain. No one knows who the Old Ones were. They left no trace of their presence in these parts except for the pictographs and petroglyphs."

"With the opening hidden by fallen rocks like it was," Vala put in, "we might be the first people to see those pictures since the Ndee found them."

"I'd say the Ndee covered the opening to keep the pictographs safe. That was no accidental rock fall." Bram spoke like he knew. "We'll all take one more look and then we're going to put the rocks back like we found them. This is a sacred place."

He spoke so solemnly he raised the hair on Vala's nape. Davis's expression was one of pure awe.

"Mokesh wanted me to see those pictures." Davis was almost whispering. "He gave me the map 'cause he wanted me to see the Old Ones' sacred place."

"I think you're right," Vala told her son.

No one complained about the hard work it took to replace the rocks so no vestige of the opening showed. As they finished, the sun came out for the first time since the rain of yesterday.

"See," Davis said. "the spirits are thanking us."

Vala decided not to correct him.

They rested and ate afterward in silence until Bram finally spoke. "Davis asked me once how I knew so much about the Ndee and I didn't answer. The truth is I'm Ndee and I've learned on this trip that there's no need to conceal what I am. There's never been any need, but I didn't understand until now."

"You're really Ndee? Honest and truly?" Davis could hardly contain his excitement.

"Half. But still Ndee. My father was a full-blood."

The father he never mentioned when he was young, Vala thought. How wonderful Bram had opened his heart and embraced his heritage.

"I'm happy for you," she told him.

He looked puzzled for a moment, then smiled and nodded. "By following Mokesh's map, I found not only the pictographs but my own treasure."

"I wish *I* was Ndee," Davis said.

"You don't need to be," Bram told him. "Ancestry isn't important unless you're ashamed to admit to it. Then it's a stone hung around your neck."

"Yeah, but it'd be so cool to be a shaman, like Mokesh."

"Who said you had to be Native American to learn what the shamans know?"

Davis blinked, obviously thinking that one over.

Bram had been so good for Davis, Vala told herself. He encouraged the boy, praised him when he did a good job, told him he was smart and treated him like a friend. She could see the difference in her son in just this short time. Not that she didn't do all those things, but the problem was in Davis's eyes she was just Mom, the person who loved you no matter what. Bram didn't have to like him.

Bram was a man Davis could look up to, and encouragement from him meant so much more than Mom's praise. She hoped some of it would stick with Davis when they returned to New York.

Davis had found worthwhile treasure, too, on this trip. He was beginning to discover he could be valued for himself. And Vala's treasure? She shook her head. She was the only holdout in the group, unless she counted learning to ride a horse.

"Time to get started on the return trip," Bram announced. "Want to bet it'll take a lot less time going down than it did coming up?"

"Aw, everyone knows that," Davis scoffed. "Wanna bet I won't get lost and get stuck full of stickers on the way back?"

"I'd say that was a given," Vala told him.

"Will we get to stop and see Pauline?" Davis asked.

Bram shook his head. "We're taking the shortest way down so you guys will have time to make your return flight. We won't be anywhere near Pauline's."

Davis looked at Vala. "I almost forgot we have to go back to New York," he said.

"That's where home is." She meant her words to come out light and cheerful, but to her own ears her tone sounded forced.

No more warm days—at least not until spring. No more nights of sleeping under the stars. No more Bram.

"Arizona's more fun than New York," Davis complained.

"That's because we're on vacation," Vala said firmly. "Vacations are always more fun."

"I'll sure miss you, Bram." Davis spoke wistfully.

Vala held her breath, hoping Davis wouldn't put Bram on the spot by asking an embarrassing question like was he going to come and see them. Of course he wasn't. She'd known that from the beginning.

"This was an exceptional trip all right," Bram said, noncommittally.

To Vala's great relief, Davis subsided.

By the time they camped that night, though, Davis had stocked up on questions.

"Is this something we can't ever talk about? I mean I know we have to keep the sacred place a secret forever and ever, but can I tell people I saw real pictographs?"

"No reason you can't," Bram said. "There are National Park sites where everyone's allowed to go and view the Old Ones' drawings."

"So if I just say somewhere in Arizona that's okay?"

"Yup."

"I sure wish Mokesh was still alive so I could tell him."

"He knows."

Davis stared at Bram. "Do you really think so?"

"Yup."

Vala didn't see any reason for a reality check. After all, how could anyone be sure Mokesh, wherever he was, didn't know?

"Sometimes you sound just like in one of those old cowboy movies," Davis commented.

"I learned my yup and nope from Gary Cooper in one of those old westerns," Bram admitted. "The people I guide expect stuff like that and it gets to be a habit."

"It must be neat to guide people. You get to ride horses and camp out and all."

"Beats sitting in an office or in court," Bram said. "You have to remember, though, that I always have another profession to fall back on if I have to. That's the important thing. Sometimes, to do what you enjoy doing, you need to have a backup plan. I'm glad I went through law school—learned a lot, made some good friends."

"I suppose." Davis didn't sound convinced.

"Take you, now," Bram went on. "A smart kid like you, you're college material. By the time you're old enough to go to college, chances are you'll have a pretty good idea of what profession appeals the most to you."

"Being a guide sounds like more fun."

"Okay," Bram said, "but college first."

"You better believe it," Vala said to her son.

After Davis called it a night, Vala and Bram sat

next to each other on his sleeping bag, close but not touching. Overhead, the waning moon scudded across the sky playing hide-and-seek with the clouds.

"Thanks for giving Davis good advice," she said.

"I lucked onto it. My mother wanted me to go to college, partly because she never had. My father's advice tended to be more philosophical, in the vein of Joseph Campbell's 'Follow your bliss.' "

"Which you did."

He half-smiled. "No. I'm just starting to try to do that now."

Vala realized he must mean his belated acknowledgment of half his heritage. "I was never quite sure exactly what Campbell meant by that," she said. "I have no driving urge to follow any road."

"That's because of Davis. You feel focusing on him is the single most important thing in your life."

Did she? Certainly that was true before she came back to Arizona and met Bram again. Her son was important to her, yes, but Bram had made her realize she was missing out on another vital part of life.

"I'm all Davis has." No way did she intend to mention that she'd learned she needed to be a woman as well as a mother.

He nodded. "There is that."

Did this man realize how easy he was to talk to? Did he entertain the slightest notion that she didn't have a clue how she was going to cope when he was thousands of miles away from her?

"You have to keep in mind not to overdo the mothering, though," Bram went on. "Davis is more capable than you may realize."

She'd learned that from watching how Bram dealt with her son. As much as she loved Davis, maybe she hadn't been doing the best by him. Surely she hadn't been influenced by Neal's put-downs of the boy—inept, clumsy, timid, whiny, useless? She fervently hoped not. Davis was always better when he was out from under his father's critical eye, but on this trip he'd proved he was none of the things his father had accused him of.

"I do try to remember he's not my baby anymore," she said.

"Keep in mind he didn't go to pieces when he was lost and hurting from the cactus spines. And remember he faced down a rattler without getting bit, because he knew how to act. I don't lie to kids. I tell him he's smart because he is—smart and brave."

"Smart enough so he's probably peeking through the flap in the tent right now seeing if we're going to kiss good night again."

"In that case, why disappoint him?"

Before she could say yes, no or maybe, she was in Bram's arms being thoroughly kissed.

As always, she lost herself in pleasure, her heart telling her this was where she belonged.

He released her far too soon to suit her, saying,

"If we go on with this the kid'll get a sex education he definitely doesn't need at his age. I remember nine as a relatively naive time in my life. Sure, I knew men and women had sex, but I didn't apply that knowledge to my mother and father. Not *them.*"

Vala sighed and nodded. "You're right. The possibility that my mother and father could be sexual beings was the farthest thing from my mind."

He took her hand and held it in his, making her feel warm and comforted. And still a bit turned on, but she tried to quash that.

"Really, why didn't you ever get married?" she asked after a time.

He grinned at her. "No one asked me."

She squeezed his fingers. "Seriously."

"My folks, I guess. I know it wasn't easy for my mother to be alone so much. I blamed my father, not realizing until lately that it might have been lonesome for him, too. Marriage looked like a painful proposition to me, one I didn't want any part of.

"You were never even tempted?"

Bram shook his head.

She decided that had been a dumb question. He probably could have any woman he wanted without benefit of marriage. And did have? Best to leave that one alone, she told herself.

"Never mind that people all around me got divorces," she said, "I had the illusion that marriage was forever, like my folks'. Otherwise I probably wouldn't have stayed with Neal as long as I did. He was not good for my ego, just as he isn't for Davis's."

"He sounds charming." Bram's voice was a near growl.

She shouldn't throw all the blame on Neal. She hadn't been what he'd expected he was getting any more than he'd been what she thought he was. But he'd been so nasty about the whole thing that it felt good to vent her feelings.

"That's all past," she said firmly. "I've no intention of making another mistake like that."

"No more marriages?"

"Something of the sort. Men are—unpredictable."

"*Men* are?" He turned to look at her, eyebrows raised. "It's women who hold the honors in that field."

She frowned and pulled her hand free of his. "Do you find me unpredictable?"

"Haven't been around you that long," he said.

"Cop-out and you know it."

"Okay, so it is," he said. "Let's take when we were kids, that night I came over to your house. You don't think the way you acted was unpredictable? It sure felt that way to me."

"Only because you didn't know what I'd overheard. And misinterpreted, as it turned out. What had you predicted? That I'd let you kiss me?"

"Hell, I can't remember. I *did* want to kiss you, though."

"And I'll bet you figured once that was accomplished I'd fall at your feet and become your willing slave?"

He grinned. "Hey, I was a hormone-driven teenager."

Vala couldn't help but wonder if the scenario she'd presented could actually have happened if she hadn't overheard the Ice Maiden conversation. She'd been totally fascinated with Bram as a teen. Of course, her parents probably would have put a stop to any relationship between them before things got to that point.

"We'll have to throw out the teen years," she admitted. "No one that young is totally reasonable."

"No one caught up in infatuation is reasonable, no matter how old they are," Bram countered.

"I like to think the years have added a little sense," she replied.

"My grandmother, my father's mother, lived well into her nineties," Bram said. "Sharp to the end. Before she died, I went to see her. I made the mistake of asking her what she'd learned from life." He shook his head. "I should have remembered about the Ndee. As Davis complained, Mokesh never explained. That's definitely a Ndee trait. Grandmother looked me in the eye and said, 'Boy, you ask a foolish question. The older we get, the more we understand we know nothing.' "

Vala took time to think that one over.

"So," Bram went on, "why are we sitting here

arguing when we actually know nothing, but just think we do?"

She smiled at him. "Because we're not yet ninety, I guess, so we don't believe it."

He was going to miss Vala. Every other time he'd been involved in a relationship with a woman, sex had been the center and the talk had been trivial.

Vala was a woman you could actually talk to and enjoy the conversation. What she said even made him think.

He'd be lying to himself if he didn't admit sex was also involved. Involved? A wimpy damn word for what was between them, physically and otherwise. He'd never gotten in this deep before, never felt the overwhelming urge to protect a particular woman from any possible harm. Hell, he was even tempted to take on that bastard of an ex-husband and punch his lights out.

Insanity.

"You look positively ferocious," Vala said. "Since you're not aiming it at me, who's the scowl for?"

"That damned Trickster," he muttered. "He can't stand to see a man get his life where he wants it without jumping in to interfere."

"If I were as old and wise as your grandmother," she said, "I might be able to answer that. In fact, I'll give it a whirl, anyway. Stasis."

"Stasis?"

"The Trickster doesn't like stasis, so he devises

ways to force change on us poor humans who keep struggling to maintain the status quo."

Bram nodded. "I'd say that's an answer worthy of a Ndee."

Vala felt absurdly complimented. She also felt sleepy. "It must be getting late," she murmured.

"You could bring your sleeping bag out here next to mine," he said. "Nothing wrong with sleeping under the stars together."

Though tempted, Vala shook her head. To preserve her sanity, she was better off sharing the tent with Davis. Because of her constant need to touch and be touched by Bram, lying next to him at night was just not a good idea. Even though that was exactly what she longed to do.

"Not tonight, but maybe once more before the trip ends," she conceded, needing that promise for herself.

TWELVE

In each night camp as they came down out of the mountains, Vala expected Davis to decide to sleep outside under the stars with Bram. Instead, her son sought the tent shortly after dark each night and didn't emerge until morning.

Which left her alone with Bram for some time before she retired to the tent. She both looked forward to those times as well as being apprehensive about them. But Bram's willpower was apparently equal to hers and all they did was talk. No more good night kisses.

Then, on the morning of the third day of the return journey, Bram announced, "Tonight'll be our last camp out. Tomorrow morning we'll be heading for home."

"Bummer," Davis muttered.

Vala felt the same. She didn't want the trip to be over.

Tonight, she vowed, I'll risk sleeping outside next to Bram. We're adults. We can control ourselves so that we're just two companions sharing the last night together under the stars. I want that last night with him.

To distract herself from thinking about how she'd feel when she was on the jet lifting away from Phoenix, Vala deliberately concentrated on the growth along the trail. Catclaw, creosote bush, jojoba, prickly pear cactus, staghorn cholla. Until this trip into the Superstitions she'd never realized there was such a variety of cacti and shrubs in this arid area.

The most spectacular was the saguaro cactus that grew all around Phoenix, looking like a giant man with his arms raised. With her eyes now accustomed to the lush greenery of the east coast, though, what did grow here seemed exotic enough to have come from another planet.

When they stopped to rest the horses, Davis said, "Look, there's a chuckwalla. He doesn't seem scared of us at all."

"As lizards go," Bram said, "chuckwallas are among the slowest and most phlegmatic."

"And the drabbest," Vala added. "Sort of a nothing color."

"Maybe 'cause he's slow he needs to sort of blend into the rocks and the ground so predators won't see him." Davis pointed at the sky. "Like that big hawk up there. I bet he eats lizards."

"Anything he can catch," Bram affirmed.

"All that makes me glad we're at the top of the food chain," Vala said.

"That's what you think," Davis put in. "Humans aren't at the top."

"Okay, I'll bite," Bram said. "What is?"

"Bite, that's a good one," Davis whooped, going into gales of laughter. When he was able to speak, he said, "What's at the top of the food chain? Vampires!"

Bram struck his forehead with the heel of his hand in mock horror while Vala rolled her eyes, chuckling.

By the time they remounted and continued on, though, her lightheartedness faded and vanished, replaced by a gloomy feeling of impending loss.

Davis, ahead of her in the single file chain, glanced back at her, but she couldn't muster up a smile.

Moments later he called to her. "Hey, Mom, we could sing like we did on the way up. You start."

What a turn of events, she thought. We arrived in Arizona with me trying to cheer Davis up and now that we're about to leave, he's trying to make *me* feel better.

She began with the old tried and true "Comin' Round The Mountain."

Davis chose one of his camp songs she and Bram had learned from him on the upward journey. Then Bram picked "Home On The Range."

The singing carried her along until their throats got too dry to continue. In one way it was a good thing the trip was near the end because they were almost out of water. And food, as well. Bram had packed for extra days but, as he'd said, he hadn't expected the trip to take so long.

Neither had she. And now she wished it had taken even longer.

Bram was well aware they could make it to Brenden's by dark, but he knew neither Vala nor Davis realized that. So, okay, he was cheating, so what? He needed this one last night with Vala. He'd long ago decided not to accept any fee at all from her, so one more night didn't make any difference. She and Davis would still have time to catch their flight the day after tomorrow.

He wished Vala and he could spend this last night alone together, but he was willing to take what he could get. Which, with Davis around, would be her company and maybe a good night kiss. He liked the kid—was going to miss him. Still, having a nine-year-old with them did put a crimp in romance.

He began looking early for the perfect spot to camp, needing to find one before they got too close to the flat. Old sharp eyes Davis might well pick up on his ruse if the kid realized they were practically out of the mountains.

Along the trail a ways, he found a clear area with a few small palo verde trees growing on one side. "This is it," he announced. "The last night's camp."

The kid had gotten so good at setting up that

Bram didn't have to tell him anything as they worked together. "I'd take you on as trail-help any day," Bram told him.

Davis beamed at the praise; then his smile faded. "Wish I could be," he said wistfully.

Bram cobbled together what remained of the food for the evening meal. "We'll have a late breakfast tomorrow at Brenden's Bronco Corral to make up for this," he told them.

When everything was clean and put away, they sat on their sleeping bags in the gathering dusk in silence.

"How about a story?" Bram said finally. "Ought to be your turn, Davis."

"I guess so." The boy sounded far from enthusiastic. Then he brightened. "Maybe one Pauline told me, okay? It's about Wind Dancer."

He began telling about a young Ndee maiden and a young warrior who couldn't speak, but could sing, and how this warrior named Wind Dancer saved the girl from a wolf.

"She was hurt pretty bad, but he cured her by singing a magic song into her ear. They fell in love and were gonna get married, but then the warriors had to go and find some of the women who got trapped in a snowstorm. Wind Dancer tried to save the women from a bear that he fought single-handed. He and the bear fell over a cliff and they all knew he'd been killed.

"It was so far down, they couldn't go get his body. When they came back into camp with the rescued women, Wind Dancer wasn't with them and so everyone mourned, especially the girl who was gonna marry him.

"But pretty soon spring came and the girl was happy again. Some of the women followed her to find out why. They found her sitting in the wild-flowers while a tiny little bird fluttered near her ear, like it was whispering to her. It was a hummingbird with feathers colored like the clothes the warrior who couldn't talk had worn. Then they knew Wind Dancer had come back to the girl he loved."

Davis glanced from Bram to Vala before adding. "There's a little bit more, but that's all I'm gonna tell tonight."

Bram wondered why. Deciding not to pry, he said, "That'd be a sad story if it didn't end like it does."

"Do you know what comes after?" Davis asked.

Bram shook his head. "No, the story of Wind Dancer, the Hummingbird, was one I hadn't heard before."

Looking relieved, Davis said, "It's your turn now."

Bram said, "I know Mokesh told you Coyote stealing Fire was the first Coyote story, but my father told me the one about Coyote and the Wild Geese came first. So it won't really be out of turn if I tell that one."

"I guess not," Davis said.

So Bram told the story of how Coyote told the

Wild Geese how much he admired their ability to fly and couldn't they help him to fly with them just once? Flattered, they lent him feathers and so he flew with the Geese for a while.

"But Coyote had his own plan, one he kept hidden. As they flew, the Geese told Coyote never to look down while flying or he'd fall. Claiming he might forget, he wheedled a magic word from them that would keep him from being hurt if he did fall.

"So when they flew over the place where Coyote had wanted to get to all along, the Fireflies' camp, he looked down and, sure enough, he began falling. Just in time he said the magic word and so he landed safely. After he took off his feathers, he began scheming how to steal Fire from the Fireflies."

Bram looked at Davis. "Know what this is supposed to teach Ndee kids?"

"I'm not sure."

"Vala?"

"How about don't believe the stranger who says he wants to fly with you just for fun."

Bram smiled. "Not bad."

Davis tugged at his ear. "Um—don't give away all your secrets?"

"Pretty good, too. My version is, if you already know someone is a Trickster—beware."

"Maybe that really is the first Coyote story," Davis said, " 'cause it comes before he steals Fire."

"I hope you don't expect a story from me," Vala said. "I haven't got any in stock unless you want to regress to something like 'The Three Billy Goats Gruff.' "

"You lucked out, Mom," Davis told her. "It's getting time for me to head for the tent."

Bram watched him haul his sleeping bag toward the tent, wondering if it wasn't a bit suspicious that Davis seemed so agreeable about going to bed early. As he recalled, it hadn't been that way on the trip in. Nor had the kid wanted to sleep outside again after that first time. Most kids loved the idea.

Dismissing the problem, he turned to Vala. "I always sort of rooted for the troll under the bridge instead of the goats," he told her.

She shook her head. "I might have known."

Bram eased back on his sleeping bag until he was stretched out. Looking up at the sky, he said, "We're down to a half moon."

He was surprised when Vala copied his move and, lying flat on her own sleeping bag, gazed at the sky. "That makes it easier to see the stars," she murmured. "Which is good, since I'm planning to sleep under them tonight."

He raised up on an elbow to stare at her and she smiled at him. "The operative word is sleep," she added.

Bram grinned, ridiculously elated. "Surely you don't think I'd be concealing a secret plan that might interfere with your sleep."

"You said it yourself. When you know someone's a Trickster—beware."

"When have I done anything even remotely Coyote-like?"

"You do have a way with you. I have a mental vision of you up there flying with the Wild Geese. Just remember, those who play with fire get burned."

"You're telling me that too late." He'd meant the words to sound teasing. Instead he heard truth ring through them.

They stared at one another. He didn't know about her, but suddenly he could scarcely breathe. His heart pounded as though he was running for his life. There was nothing on earth he wanted more than to make love with Vala. Now.

He started to reach for her when, floating up from the flat land below, came the plaintive wail of a coyote.

Vala, listening to the coyote's call, swallowed, struggling to force out words to help break the spell she and Bram were caught in. "See," she managed to say, hearing the telltale huskiness in her voice with dismay. "I was right about the Trickster all along. He's out there somewhere laughing."

Bram, who'd been up on an elbow, sank back down onto his back, muttering, "You can bet he's the only one who is."

Neither of them said anything else for some time. Vala told herself it might be best if she retreated to the tent, but she didn't move. Gazing up at the stars, she saw instead the twin lights of a jet heading for a landing in Phoenix. Soon she'd be on another, heading up, up and away from Arizona.

Blinking back tears, she fought to focus on something else. All that came to mind was her son's story of Wind Dancer. "I wonder what was at the end of that story about the hummingbird and why Davis didn't want to tell us," she said.

"Who knows?" Bram's tone was flat. Meaning he didn't care?

"Davis and Pauline shared secrets," she went on, not caring either, but needing to keep her mind locked onto something innocuous.

"He's lucky. Pauline doesn't take to everybody."

"I could see that." Gratefully she hung onto this new topic. "She's definitely one of a kind. I can't imagine her living in a city."

In a way, Bram, too, seemed more suited to the wilds than to city life. Perhaps he lived on a ranch outside of town somewhere. "Where in Phoenix do you live?" she asked.

"In a suburban house a grateful client sold me. Nice guy, good price. There were some compensations to being a lawyer."

"Do you like living in the city?"

"As long as I can have nights under the stars like this, I don't mind," he said. "I must have inherited some of my mother's genes along with my father's wanderlust because I enjoy having a place to come home to. Strange, I never figured to settle in like I have."

"Maybe it's due to Sheba. They say a cat turns a house into a home."

He chuckled. "Overturns a house is more like it with her. Or was. I can't believe how the kittens have changed my wild and carefree feline into a sedate mother."

"Kids do that to mothers," she said.

"Not all mothers," he told her with wicked suggestiveness threading through his words. "No way would I describe you as sedate."

"Remember, I'm on vacation," she said defensively, secretly thrilled with his insinuation that he'd enjoyed the wild moments they'd shared. He couldn't know he was the only man who'd ever tempted her into forgetting everything but him.

"We'd all enjoy ourselves more if we could think of living as a lifelong vacation."

"Fat chance. The necessity to earn a living is no vacation, even if you like what you do." She sighed. "Actually my job's okay. It's just that I hate to—" She broke off, not wanting to reveal any more of her feelings than she already had.

"Why don't you and Davis spend tomorrow night at my place?" Bram said. "There's plenty of room and I know he'll want to pick out his kitten."

Damn the man—he'd set that up so she couldn't refuse. Instead of answering, she said, "Are you really up to the trouble of shipping the kitten to him when it's old enough?"

"I keep my promises." He sounded offended.

"Well, in that case, we accept your kind offer of

shelter." She deliberately brought Davis into her answer, letting Bram know she was on to his manipulative ways.

Not that she didn't want to spend the extra time with him, but she feared it would make leaving all the more difficult.

"Are you disappointed there was no Apache gold at the end of the trail?" he asked.

She thought about what she'd found instead. Not the pictographs, awesome though they were. She *had* discovered something, after all: She'd learned that not all men were like Neal. Bram, at least, treated lovemaking as the wonder it could be. He was tender and passionate and he made her feel as desirable as if she were the most beautiful woman in the world.

He'd given her back her sexuality. Not that it would do her much good, since, unfortunately, she didn't want to make love with any other man except Bram. There *were* no other men like Bram.

Careful, girl, she warned herself, you sound like a woman in love.

A moment later, she caught her breath as a realization struck her. She *was* in love with him. With Bram. She made an inarticulate sound of disbelief and anger. How had she let that happen?

"What's the matter?" he asked. "You okay?"

No, she wasn't okay: she doubted if she ever would be again. "The truth hurts," she muttered.

"Been known to happen," he agreed. "Care to share this particular truth with me?"

"No!" she snapped.

She certainly had no intention of embarrassing them both by blurting out she was in love with him. He'd more or less told her his preference was for brief affairs, no strings attached. Love certainly hadn't entered his mind and, for her own peace of mind, she shouldn't have allowed it room in hers.

"You still owe me a story," he said after a long silence.

"I what?"

"Davis told a story, I told a story—it's your turn. And you don't get off the hook by saying you don't know any."

"I already told you it would have to be the three goats and the troll or nothing."

"I don't buy that. I'm willing to bet you have a storehouse of family stories. Think about it. Was the gold ring tale the only one your Grandmother Ella ever told you?"

"You wouldn't be interested in family stuff."

"Try me."

"Well, now that I think about it, there is something. My grandmother had a sister named Letty, who was older. I wasn't meant to know about this at all; it's an overheard tale. And I wasn't eavesdropping. I was a kid playing with my little cars underneath the dining room table where it was like a cave with the tablecloth hanging down all around me.

"Little cars?" he asked. "You played with cars?"

"They were left over from when my father was

a boy. He gave them to me and I loved them. Anyway, the dining room was an ell off the living room where my mother and grandmother were sitting and talking. They had no idea I was under the table when my mother asked why no one ever mentioned Aunt Letty.

"At the time, I didn't even know there was a Letty in the family, so I perked up my ears and began listening. At first my grandmother didn't seem inclined to tell her but my mother persisted.

" 'She may have been my own sister,' Grandmother said, 'but when she did what she did, I felt I had never known her. Not at all. Of course, our parents disowned her and took all her pictures out of the albums. After that, they never again mentioned her name in my hearing.'

" 'Good heavens, what did Letty do?' my mother asked.

"I didn't understand all they were saying but I stored the information away and pieced it together when I got old enough to know what some of the words meant. It seems Letty had been offered a job in Las Vegas when all the casinos except one or two were downtown and the mob ran all of them. I guess their parents assumed she was working as a secretary or something like that. Times had been hard on their Iowa farm and they appreciated the money she sent home from time to time.

"Ella was sent wonderful presents, too, and could hardly wait to grow up so she could join her sister in Nevada. None of them had any clue what was going on until Letty made headlines."

"Don't tell me she was a showgirl."

"I won't, because she wasn't. Actually, it was clear from the newspaper stories that early on she'd become what Grandmother Ella called 'a fallen woman, and for money, yet,' before she took up with one of the lesser mobsters."

"A gun moll. Fascinating."

"Gun is right—she shot the man. The news stories played it up as a jealousy murder, since she also wounded the 'other woman.' Apparently Letty was let out on bail before the case came to trial because less than a week later she suffered a fatal 'accident' while crossing the street. According to Ella the entire family was relieved.

"It never occurred to any of them that she'd probably been murdered by the mob so she wouldn't have a chance to spill anything she might know. It's hard to believe my great-grandparents could have been so narrow-minded and so innocent."

"Different times," Bram said. "That's quite a story. You're the first person I've known with a notorious great-aunt hidden in her background."

"I've never told anyone else her story. Since I've gone this far, I might as well admit that I've always sort of admired her. Not for murdering the man, but for striking out on her own and surviving any way she could in a setting and a time really hostile to women. If Davis had been a girl, I think I might have named him Letty."

"Interesting she was let out on bail. That's unusual in a murder case where there's a witness—in this case, the other woman. No doubt the mob knew who to bribe to get her free long enough to off her."

"I never thought of that. How cold-blooded." Vala shivered.

Evidently Bram saw this because he said, "Getting cold?" Without waiting for an answer he sat up and pulled her over onto his sleeping bag where he put an arm around her, nestling her against his side. "Better?"

"Umm," she murmured. "If I were Sheba, I'd purr."

For a few moments, Bram was content just to have her close to him, but it didn't last long until desire began to override every other emotion. He shifted, turning her face up to him and kissed her.

Her lips were soft and welcoming, she tasted of herself with a slight chocolate overlay from the last bar in the supplies—he'd split it three ways as dessert. Much as he liked chocolate, her flavor was far more addictive.

That's what it was—addiction. He was addicted to Vala. Would he ever be able to kick the habit? Not wanting to think about that just now, he concentrated on the kiss, deepening it, feeling her eager response rage through him.

Davis is in the tent, he warned himself. Don't let this get out of hand.

He wouldn't; all he wanted was to hold her in his arms for a while, to kiss and caress her. No, that was a damn lie. What he wanted was to possess her completely and have her possess him as well. He needed to be locked with her in an embrace that would send them both on a trip to the stars.

Vala was unique—no other woman was like her, or even came close. She not only aroused him almost past bearing, but she also made him aware of his own strength, strength he could and would use to protect her, to keep her safe always.

"Sweet Vala," he whispered against her lips. "My beautiful Vala. Mine."

The last word echoed in his mind, mocking him. No matter how many times he might say it, she wasn't his.

"Bram," she breathed. "We can't."

No, they couldn't, not under the circumstances. But he let her go reluctantly.

After they'd bedded down, each with a sleeping bag partially zipped up, she reached a hand to him and he grasped it. He half-smiled, thinking he'd never in his life believed he'd be lying next to a woman he needed in the worst way and do nothing more than hold her hand.

When he finally started to drift off, a stray thought floated across his mind. When he first set eyes on the kitten yowling at his front door, he had

208

Jane Anderson

no intention of keeping her, none at all. A pet anchored you down. He needed to be free, needed no restrictions, no responsibilities. He still felt that way. Didn't he?

Maybe. But, for better or for worse, somehow Sheba had become his cat. He wouldn't dream of parting with her.

Half-asleep, he didn't quite manage to make the connection between Sheba and Vala.

THIRTEEN

Bram roused in the morning to Davis's voice saying, "Aren't you guys ever gonna wake up? I already got the tent down by myself."

Glancing at Vala, Bram saw her blinking drowsily. "Morning," she mumbled.

"I figure the sooner we get going," Davis said, "the sooner we get breakfast at Brenden's Bronco Corral."

Bram yawned and stretched. "Right as usual," he told Davis.

Since Vala had slept in her clothes, she had nothing to do but slide out and reach for her socks and boots. Bram, though, had stripped down to his shorts. In deference to Davis's modesty where Vala was concerned, he said, "All females present turn your backs," before emerging and reaching for his jeans.

Her smile was amused when she turned to look at him after he sounded the all clear.

"Gee," she said as they saddled up, "I worked danged hard learning all this stuff about horses and now the trip's almost over. It isn't a skill I'll need to use back in New York, you know."

"You always tell me nothing learned is ever wasted," Davis pointed out.

"Good advice always comes back to haunt you," Bram told her with a grin.

"Everything I brought along is dirty, including me," she said to him as they started off. "I hope you've got a washer and dryer."

"How come you're asking Bram that, Mom?"

"Sorry, I forgot to tell you. Bram's invited us to spend tonight at his place."

"You mean I get to see the kittens? Cool."

"You can pick the one you want," Bram reminded him. "Even name it. I'll ship your kitten to you later."

They soon came out onto the flat. If either Davis or Vala realized the night camp hadn't been necessary, neither said so. Could be they both, like him, hated to see the trip end.

Once they reached Brenden's, Bram told Mac about the packhorse going lame. "Seems okay now, but you might want to check him."

He then took Mac aside and told him privately that the bill for the horses was to go to him, unlike the customary arrangement of being paid for by the person who'd hired him. Mac raised an eyebrow, but said nothing.

After they ate, Vala thanked Mac for choosing Susie Q for her. "She's the only horse that could ever have put up with me," she told him.

"Figured you wasn't much of a rider," he said.

When she asked about paying him, he told her it'd been taken care of. Vala glanced at Bram inquisitively and he smiled. He'd explain later.

Again, Davis asked to ride in his pickup and Vala gave her permission.

"We'll swing by the airport so you can get rid of that rental car," Bram suggested. "It's on the way to my place. I can just as well take you there tomorrow to catch your flight."

When Vala hesitated, he added, "I'm planning to see you off anyway."

She agreed and followed him to the airport. At the rental return, while Bram was transferring the last suitcase from the car to his pickup, he overheard the attendant ask Vala if she was planning to fly out today.

"No," she said. "Tomorrow."

"Reason I asked," the man went on, "is I figure maybe you ain't heard they plan on shutting down a lot of the airports east of us on account of that winter storm."

"Thanks, I didn't know about that," she told him. "Surely things will be better tomorrow."

The man shook his head. "You better call and make sure in the morning. They say it's some storm."

"You mean we might get stranded here?" Davis asked. "Yay!"

Bram kept his mouth shut but couldn't squelch a pleased smile.

Vala frowned, saying something about if she was delayed, she hoped she'd still have a job when she got back. "My boss wasn't too thrilled about giving me this time off," she finished.

"I wouldn't care if we never went back," Davis said. "I like Arizona."

Sitting between Bram and Vala in the pickup, he chattered most of the way to their destination, pointing out sights along the way and asking questions.

Vala listened to her son with half an ear. The news about the storm had upset her a little—mostly because the delay was only that. A delay. She'd still have to go back to New York sooner or later. All it really meant would be a prolonged goodbye instead of a quick closure.

"Mom?" Davis said. "You look cross."

She blinked. "I'm not. I'm just a little worried about getting home."

"What for? We're gonna be at Bram's house, not that crummy motel."

"I thought you liked the motel pool," she was provoked into saying.

"You weren't listening. Bram's got a pool. And a Jacuzzi. And he's gonna find his guitar and maybe teach me to play."

She glanced across at Bram. "All in one day?"

He shrugged. "Who knows? Maybe we'll get lucky and the storm'll hang on for a week."

"You two are impossible."

"Come on," Bram coaxed. "Admit you can't wait to soak in the Jacuzzi."

Since she'd been thinking how good that would feel, she gave him a reluctant grin, then turned back to the window, firmly repressing any visions of Bram stripped down for the Jacuzzi. She concentrated on the passing scene.

How Phoenix had changed since she'd lived here! Much larger for one thing—there didn't seem to be any end to the city sprawl. But, compared to the east coast cities where the winter turned everything drab and dingy a week after a snowfall, Phoenix looked bright and colorful.

With the sun's warmth coming through the open windows of the pickup cab, it was hard to believe a storm was closing airports across the rest of the country. Since there was nothing she could do to change what was happening, she decided to relax and enjoy whatever extra time she might have to spend here.

One thing was certain—Davis was happy about it. Bram, too, seemed pretty enthusiastic about spending more time in their company. And the truth was she couldn't really say she was sorry.

She looked at her son. "Once we get to Bram's, first things first, kid."

He eyed her resignedly. "I suppose that means I got to take a shower right away. Even before I see the kittens?"

"You know it."

"Happens I have two showers," Bram put in, slanting a wicked glance at Vala.

"Being a gentleman, I'm sure you'd allow me to use yours first," she said as demurely as she could. "But I'll wait until Davis takes his shower and then use that one."

Not long after this, Bram left the freeway via an off ramp and turned onto a residential street.

"Look at all the orange trees right in people's yards," Davis said.

"Arizona grapefruit are better than Arizona oranges," Bram cautioned. "The oranges tend to be bitter."

After a few blocks he entered a dead-end street and pulled into a driveway, hitting the garage door opener as he did. When the door lifted, he parked next to a sporty-looking silver BMW already in the garage.

Seeing her looking at it, he said, "What I use on those rare occasions when I have to remember I'm a lawyer."

Vala smiled. "I suppose you keep the necktie in the car."

They entered the house through a connecting door and were immediately confronted by a vocal Sheba. She twined around Bram's legs, assessing them with her beautiful blue eyes.

"She sounds like she's scolding you," Davis told Bram.

"Right. She's annoyed because I dared to go

away and leave her." He lifted the cat into his arms and she immediately climbed onto his shoulder.

"Neato," Davis said.

Bram led them to the two guest rooms, which shared a bathroom, and Vala shooed Davis into the shower there, telling him she'd lay out clean clothes on his bed. Thank heaven she'd left one clean set in the car for each of them to go home in.

But later, once she was dressing after finishing her own shower, she fingered her clothes with distaste. True, she'd packed this navy blue pants suit so she'd be comfortable on the plane, but it was so—so New York.

She longed for a brightly colored cotton skirt to wear with the white short-sleeved sweater she'd packed, and maybe a scarf with the same colors in it as the skirt.

Eyeing herself in the mirror as she blow-dried her hair, she frowned at the colorless combination of navy blue pants and white top. She looked— efficient. Even on the trail, though she'd been no style setter, she'd come off with more zip than this.

Emerging from the bedroom, she followed the sound of Davis's voice and found him with Bram, sitting on the floor beside a box where Sheba nestled among her nursing kittens. As Vala eased down next to them, Bram took her hand and guided it toward the mother cat, allowing Sheba to smell her fingers.

"Vala's a friend," he said.

Friend. Was that what she wanted their relationship to be? His efficient friend, she thought moodily.

"Mom, did you know Siamese kittens were all white at first?" Davis asked. "Bram says they don't get their masks like their mother's got till later. These'll probably be seal points 'cause Sheba is and so was the father cat."

Gazing at the kittens, Vala saw they were, indeed, all white. "Have you chosen yours?" she asked her son.

He pointed at the one at the far end of the food line, a kitten smaller than the others. "He's mine and I'm gonna call him Zorro."

"But he's the runt." The words came out before Vala thought.

"I already know that. But Zorro needs me. The others don't."

"Zorro seems healthy enough," Bram put in. He reached in the box and gently disengaged the kitten from its mother.

Zorro let out a squeak of protest, causing Sheba to comment, but she didn't object otherwise to Bram holding her kitten.

"See, he's got a crook in his tail," Davis said, gazing at Zorro as though he was a prize winner. "His eyes are a little bit crossed, too. Those things happen sometimes in Siamese cats, Bram says."

Bram deposited the kitten in Davis's hands and the boy carefully raised Zorro until its fur brushed his cheek. The kitten reached out and sank its tiny claws into Davis's T-shirt, trying to climb onto him.

Davis smiled happily. "He likes me already."

Later, after Vala had washed, dried and folded their clothes and packed most of them, she rejoined Bram and Davis in the kitchen. They'd gone for quesadillas and enchiladas while she was busy and were laying out the food for lunch.

"We watched the TV weather channel before we left," Davis told her. "That old storm's gonna blanket New York."

"Up to a foot of snow," Bram put in. "With high winds. A regular blizzard. I called your airline and all flights to New York and New Jersey have been canceled for today and tomorrow. They'll call here to reschedule you when they can."

Vala thought she probably ought to worry, but her heart lifted. Irrationally, she wondered if there was a nearby store where she could buy the kind of skirt she craved so she wouldn't look so—staid. Before she could stop herself, she asked, "Is there a mall around here?"

"You wanna go shopping?" Davis asked incredulously. "We're going swimming after lunch."

"We could spare an hour in the mall while our lunch digests." Bram put in. "That do?"

Vala nodded.

After lunch, before they could leave, Bram's

friend Nick, the guy who'd been taking care of Sheba, showed up in full western regalia.

"Hey, Hunter," he said, after being introduced, "I was beginning to wonder if the Superstitions had got you this time, but I see I was wrong." He winked at Vala, as if they shared a joke Bram wasn't in on.

"We ran into some unforeseen delays," Bram said.

"Don't blame you a bit." Again Nick winked at her. "Well, I was going to invite you to take in the rodeo with me tomorrow—got two tickets—but . . ."

"Hang on," Bram said, then turned to Davis. "You like rodeos?"

"I've only seen them on TV," Davis said, "but sure!"

"Nick used to be a rodeo rider before he got all stove up," Bram said.

"Whoa!" Davis gazed awestuck at Nick. "You mean you rode bucking broncs and all?"

"Got to admit I did," Nick said. "Too young to know any better till I got thrown and busted my femur. That's the big bone up here in the thigh, kid. You don't ever want to break that sucker. Still got a limp."

"Yeah, and don't think he doesn't use that limp to advantage when he has a court case," Bram added.

It was Vala's turn to stare at Nick. This—cowboy was a lawyer?

"Why don't you stick around?" Bram said. "I got an extra suit; you can swim with us a little later. Meanwhile, you and Davis can get acquainted while I drive his mother to our local mall. That way you'll know each other better when you two take in the rodeo tomorrow. Not often you get a new audience for those tired old rodeo tales, amigo. Davis here is a pretty fair horseman; he'll enjoy them."

Davis glanced uncertainly at Vala.

"If you want to go to the rodeo it's all right with me," she said.

Davis looked up at Nick. "You sure you want to take me?"

"Hey, kid, I can already tell you'll be livelier company than old Hunter, here."

"Well, I'd sure like to go see a real, live rodeo."

"You're on!" Nick clapped him on the shoulder.

On the way to the mall, Vala said, "It was nice of you to ask Nick to take Davis to the rodeo. I hope your friend doesn't mind."

"Nick's divorced. He has a son a year or so younger than Davis and he doesn't get to see the kid very often, since his ex-wife lives in Virginia. He misses the boy—he'll enjoy being with Davis."

In the mall, Bram announced he wanted to look for a pet store. "Meet you at the truck in a half hour?" he asked.

"Better give me forty-five minutes."

He nodded and took off.

Vala zeroed in on a likely looking women's wear store and managed to find exactly what she was looking for. Tempted by a top that matched one of the colors in the skirt, she bought that, too.

Since she had twenty minutes left, she wandered through the mall, window-shopping. From a shoe store a pair of sandals called to her and she couldn't resist them. Then she found a book on the Ndee that she though Davis might enjoy and was on her way back to the truck when she passed a lingerie shop. Her steps slowed and she stopped. All she had to sleep in was the sweats. Clean now, but still totally utilitarian. Her nightclothes back home were much the same. Assuring herself that every woman needed at least one pretty nightgown, she stepped into the shop.

As she fingered the filmy confections on the racks, she told herself firmly she was not buying this for anyone but herself. Taken with a totally impractical blue waltz-length gown that the saleswoman insisted was the exact color of her eyes, she bought it and reached the truck only five minutes late.

By the time they returned to the house, Nick and Davis had become fast friends. Nick stayed around to swim with them before leaving, promising to pick Davis up in the morning.

Vala spent the rest of the afternoon in a languorous daze, appreciating not having to climb on Susie Q and ride. After the first couple of days she'd enjoyed the trip, but how good it was just to laze around for a change. She felt absurdly honored when Sheba strolled into the living room, talked to her for a bit and then jumped onto her lap to be petted until kitten squeaks sent the cat hurrying away.

She was dozing when Bram and Davis, who'd been tossing horseshoes in the backyard, came in.

"This son of yours has a wicked pitch," Bram told her. "Got almost as many ringers as me—and I'm an old pro."

Davis grinned so proudly that Vala had to hide the tears that sprang to her eyes. She'd always known there was nothing wrong with her son, but it was wonderful to see it proven. All because Bram was a man who cared how the boy felt.

Since Bram insisted they needed exotic food to make up for what they had to eat on the trail, supper turned out to be Chinese takeout, eaten late due to the afternoon popcorn. Cleaning up afterward took hardly any time. Davis soon settled in front of the den TV to watch a *Star Trek* video, leaving Vala and Bram alone in the living room.

"Some different from telling stories in the moonlight," he said, rising and ambling over to join her on the couch.

"I think people should do more of that," she said. "We all watch too much TV. Well, maybe you don't, since you're a guide."

"Somehow what's on the tube doesn't match

looking up at the stars." He started to reach for her hand.

At that moment, Sheba padded into the room and leaped onto the couch between them. Bram shrugged and began to pet the cat instead.

If it hadn't been Sheba, it would have been Davis wandering in to ask a question, Vala told herself. She and Bram were definitely not alone in his house. And wouldn't be, even when Davis was sound asleep in his room.

"Single mothers have to keep up appearances," she muttered, half to herself.

"Why? You think Sheba cares what you do? Remember, she's a single mother, too. Of five, yet."

"Her kittens don't care what she does as long as she feeds them. Davis is not a kitten."

"Granted. So you think it'd bother him if we held hands—is that it?"

She eyed him sideways. "Holding hands is only the beginning, not the complete story."

Bram scooped Sheba onto his lap, then pulled Vala closer and put his arm over her shoulder. "Now we can both pet her," he said.

Vala ran her fingers over the cat's soft fur and Sheba's black mask turned toward her, accompanied by a series of trills.

"Sorry," she murmured, "I don't understand Siamese cat talk. But if you mean you like it, good. Because I enjoy petting you."

"I had a feeling you were a cat woman," Bram said.

"I like dogs, too, but cats better. Maybe because they purr."

Like I'd be doing, if I knew how, Vala thought, cuddling against him. It felt so right to be here like this with Bram.

"Mom," Davis called, "I wanna get in my pjs before I watch the rest of this. Where are they?"

"On the dresser in your room," she called back, wondering if she should pull away from Bram. She decided not to. After all, her son had already seen them kiss. There was nothing wrong with a little hugging.

"That kid's a true male," Bram said. "Can't figure out where the female in his life puts things."

After a comfortable silence, she said, "You never did tell me what plans of yours I interrupted with my plea for help."

"Nothing important."

"I happened to see a Caribbean vacation brochure on the coffee table, so I wondered if maybe you'd been planning a trip."

"I took a trip, didn't I?" he asked.

"Not to the Caribbean, though. I've never been there. Have you?"

He nodded, then told her about his favorite island, St. Amaris. "It's not the tourist trap the others have become," he finished. "You'd like it."

She undoubtedly would, but her chances of getting there were slim to nonexistent. This trip would max out her credit card. Which reminded her.

She sat up straight and said, "You haven't told me what your fee will be."

"Nothing. I have no intention of charging an old friend."

Old friend? They'd hardly even been acquaintances in school.

"Thank you, but I'd rather—"

He held up a hand. "It's my belated holiday gift to you and Davis. Please accept it gracefully, the way I'm sure your mother taught you."

Put that way, he made it difficult for her to argue.

"That's very generous of you," she told him. "I know Davis will think so, too."

Sheba yawned, then stretched, leaped onto the floor and went to check her offspring.

"What a good mother," Vala said. "I imagine she'll miss the kittens when they get old enough to leave."

"Not for long, maybe a couple of days, the vet says. Cats are programmed to let their kittens fend for themselves once they're weaned and she's taught them to hunt."

"Not like humans. It can be hard for us to let go even when they turn eighteen."

Bram turned toward her and took both her hands in his. "Promise me you won't hang onto Davis like that."

Somewhat taken aback, she stared at him.

"And don't widen those big blue eyes at me," he added. "You know what I'm talking about."

"I'm just surprised you—care," she said.

"He's learning to trust himself to be competent. I can't ask you to keep him from his father, even though I think staying away from him might help the boy."

"If Neal doesn't ask to see Davis, I don't intend to push it," she said. "Davis never asks to visit him."

Sighing, she added, "I try to do what's best for him."

Bram grinned at her. "Yeah, I found that out when you insisted you knew how to ride."

She smiled. "I got appropriately punished for my lie, but all's well that ends well."

"I'd say *your* end wasn't very well for a few days there."

Davis appeared in the living room archway in his pajamas "Is it okay if I have some juice and the rest of the popcorn?" he asked, looking at Bram.

"Help yourself," Bram told him.

"Hey, you guys are holding hands," Davis said. "Cool."

Vala promptly removed her hands from Bram's, but by then Davis was gone.

"You're overreacting," Bram said.

"Maybe, but when he says something like that, it makes me feel like I shouldn't be."

"Why? Because you're his mother and mothers don't hold hands with or kiss men?"

"You make it sound ridiculous."

"Davis doesn't mind. What he says shows that."

Vala knew he was right. Davis seemed pleased she liked Bram and attributed the kiss, and probably the hand-holding as well, to that. But how he'd react to anything more wasn't clear. Not that she intended to give him any opportunity *to* react to more.

"I'm really tired," she told Bram. "A good night's sleep on a real innerspring mattress sounds like heaven right now, so I think I'll turn in early."

"And lie there wondering if I'm going to creep into your room once you're asleep and carry you off to my lair?" The amusement in his voice riled her, since something of the sort had crossed her mind.

"Or maybe hoping?" he added.

That, too, damn the man.

"Neither," she lied. "You won't and we both know it."

"Don't be too sure. You were wrong about me years ago, don't forget."

"That was in another time and in other circumstances. And I didn't really know what you were like then."

True. But if it hadn't been for that damn Ice Maiden bet she'd overheard, she certainly would have let him kiss her. At the very least.

"And you think you know me now?" he persisted.

Vala nodded.

Bram responded by yanking her to him and fitting his mouth over hers in a kiss that she felt in the very marrow of her bones.

FOURTEEN

Vala's attempt to escape from him without so much as a good night kiss had driven Bram to remind her just how potent a combination they were together. He hadn't meant to take it any farther, but the feel of Vala in his arms and the taste of her in his mouth drove him past the point he'd meant to make. Now he wanted, needed more.

Her heated response told him she felt the same way and he was close to losing control, despite the fact he could hear *Star Trek* sound effects filtering into the living room from the den, reminding him of Davis's presence. Just a little longer, he told himself, just a little more.

"Bram, please, we can't." Vala's whispered plea against his lips brought him to his senses and, very much against his will, he released her.

As he did, he realized the faint drone of sound from the den had diminished. Rising from the couch, he went to investigate. On the TV screen the credits were rolling, the movie was over. Davis lay sprawled on the floor, sound asleep.

Bram switched off the TV and set the VCR to rewind before crouching to lift Davis into his arms. He carried him into the guest bedroom, found Vala had folded back the covers earlier, and eased the boy onto the bed. He tucked him in, then brushed a stray strand of fair hair from the kid's forehead. Strange to have gotten so attached in such a short time to a child who wasn't his.

When he straightened, he saw Vala standing in the doorway watching him. The look in her eyes settled into his heart.

He wanted to hold her, to protect her, to keep her and her son from all possible harm. Which clearly meant letting her sleep alone tonight. Davis was in a strange bed, in a strange house—sound sleeper or not, there was no guarantee he wouldn't rouse and get up to make sure where his mother was.

Hell of a note when a man had the woman he wanted to make love to right here in his own house, but wasn't going to carry her off to his bed. Where had he acquired all these damn scruples anyway?

"You mentioned something about an early night," he said to her as she approached him. "Good idea." Not trusting himself to so much as touch her, he strode from the guest bedroom, tossing a "see you in the morning" over his shoulder.

Bram realized when he crawled into his bed that he was more tired than he'd thought. Good. Maybe he wouldn't lie awake imagining Vala sharing the bed with him, with the accompanying frustration because she wasn't.

Luck was with him; he fell into the deep pit of sleep almost immediately . . .

He was standing on a high plateau with a blanket wrapped around him. His long hair, hanging in braids down his back, was bound by a beaded band. He was himself and, at the same time, another.

"So we meet," a hissing voice said. He who spoke was not visible. "You, who are of the blood, take heed."

Words came to Bram, "Grandfather," he said, using the proper term for an honored elder. "Grandfather, I listen."

"Why do you not help us, you who are wise in the ways of the white man's law?"

Bram had no answer.

"Be warned," the voice continued. "It is not enough to say you are one of us. Look at me!"

Though the rock in front of him had been empty a moment ago, now a giant rattler lay coiled atop it. Mokesh, the Guardian. Aghast, Bram stared into its yellow eyes.

"Become a warrior!" The words reverberated in Bram's head.

A whirlwind swept across the rocky plateau, lifting him up and away, stripping off the blanket and the braids, leaving him naked. . . .

And naked he awoke, in his own bed, befogged by the remnants of the dream.

A vision, he seemed to hear his father say. Vision or dream, he remained shaken.

It wasn't so easy to fall asleep the second time.

Though Vala had been truly tired when she climbed into her bed, sleep remained elusive, playing hide-and-seek with her. The root of the problem was that she wanted to be elsewhere—in bed with Bram, to be specific. She yearned to be in his arms, nestled against his warm body.

Since that was not to be, she tossed and turned, changing position again and again, not finding the comfort she craved. When she finally looked at the lighted red numerals on the bedside clock, it was well after midnight.

The next she knew, someone was speaking her name. Davis? Her eyes popped open—to daylight and Bram standing over her, wearing khaki shorts and no shirt.

She sat up, looking around.

"Sleepyhead," Bram said, easing down onto the bed. "It's near eleven. Davis has already left for the rodeo with Nick. How about brunch in the Jacuzzi?"

He reached to slide the strap of her new nightgown back up onto her shoulder, his fingers warm against her skin. "Better agree in a hurry or you'll never get out of this bed."

"Um, what's for brunch?" she asked.

"A surprise," he promised. "So don't bother to get dressed."

"How about my swimsuit?"

"Woman, don't try my patience. This is a naked brunch." As he spoke, he rose and stripped off his shorts. "See?"

What she saw cleared her head of any sleep remnants.

"Meet you there." He exited, twirling the shorts on his forefinger.

Vala, shy about parading through the house with nothing on, decided not to discard her nightgown. Never mind that it didn't conceal much, she felt better wearing something.

Bram, waiting for her in the Jacuzzi, whistled when he saw her. "That gown beats those gray sweats all hollow," he said. "I almost hate to see you take it off. But, as I told you, this is a naked brunch. People with clothes on don't get to eat."

Eyeing the food spread along the edge of the sunken tub, Vala reached for the bottom of the nightgown and slowly drew it over her head. When it was off, she glanced at Bram and a thrill shot through her at the hungry look in his eyes. She eased into the warm, frothing water next to the food, excited by being naked. She'd never before done anything even remotely like this.

"I'm starved," she said, reaching for a half of grapefruit already prepared.

"So am I."

"Would you like me to pass you something?"

He shook his head, "Just eat fast."

"Mmm," she said, "this grapefruit's delicious. What did you put on it?"

"Warm honey. Can't wait to taste it—second-hand."

She shot him a mock frown and he grinned.

Though she was hungry, her need for food was rapidly falling behind her need for Bram. As she finished the grapefruit and reached for a wedge of buttered toast set on a warmer, she tried to pace herself but instead found she was eating as fast as she could.

Bram edged closer.

She poured herself a cup of coffee from the carafe to wash down the toast. After she'd taken a couple of swallows, Bram eased the cup from her hand, set it down and pulled her into his arms.

"The food can wait. I can't," he murmured against her lips before kissing her.

His taste on her lips, his scent in her nostrils, she gave herself up to pure enjoyment. She meant to savor every second of their lovemaking so she'd have something to remember during the days ahead.

Quickly pushing the thought of leaving from her mind, she wound her arms around his neck, holding him to her, his body, as slick with water as hers was, hard and infinitely arousing against hers.

She'd never made love in a Jacuzzi before and she found the water frothing around her erotic, increasing her desire as it caressed her almost as intimately as Bram was doing. Why couldn't these moments last forever?

By the time he urged her legs up until they were wrapped around his hips so they could join together, she was beyond thought, could only feel There was nothing like this, had never been anything like this, she could die of pleasure. . . .

Afterward, out of the Jacuzzi, wrapped in a towel, she reached for her nightgown only to have Bram pluck it from her and toss it away.

"But—" she protested.

"Brunch isn't over," he told her. "We've barely tasted the first course. Anyone would think you'd never explored the fascination of nakedness."

She hadn't. But she was willing to give it a spin.

He poured her another cup of coffee and took one himself. "Toast?" he asked. "It's still warm. And there's peach jam."

Naked, they sat side by side on towels, eating. Though she was hardly aware of how the food tasted, she'd never enjoyed a brunch more.

He was so good to look at—broad-shouldered and muscular without the muscles bunching up excessively. He had very little hair on his chest, perhaps due to his heritage? She viewed it as an asset. Hairy men had never appealed to her.

When he said with considerable amusement, "Find anything you like?" she realized she'd been staring and flushed.

At the same time, she saw he was becoming aroused again and shivers of anticipation coursed through her.

"Cold?" he asked, setting down his coffee cup.

Before she could deny it, he rose to his feet, grasped her hand and pulled her up. "I know the best place to warm up," he told her. "Been trying to get you in my bed ever since you set foot in the house."

His room was sparsely furnished with eclectic pieces, which, except for the bed, didn't look new but comfortably used. All in all it looked surprisingly homey. Peeling the covers back, he pulled her with him into the king-sized bed and wrapped his arms around her.

"Getting warm?" he murmured.

"You'll have to do better than that," she teased, feeling incredibly young and lighthearted.

"Think I can't?"

"I'll have to wait and see."

He proceeded to take her down paths she hadn't traveled before as he caressed every part of her body, making her mindless with need, then fulfilling that need.

She clung to him afterward, not wanting to let him go. Ever. As he held her next to him, everything seemed bathed in a golden light. She was drifting into a doze when suddenly she felt something cold probe her ear; then Sheba's distinctive voice demanded to know what they were doing.

"I thought I closed the door," Bram muttered as

the cat climbed onto him and stared into his face. "I swear she must have opened it. There's such a thing as being too smart, cat."

Sheba, once she was convinced everything was all right, decided to curl up on Bram's pillow. Her purring acted as a lullaby, easing them both into a nap.

When Bram woke, Sheba was gone. Vala, though, still lay next to him. She looked so young asleep, he almost felt he had teenaged Vala back. But he greatly preferred the woman she'd become.

He hadn't yet told her that, when he'd called the airline before he woke her, they'd given him a tentative departure time of noon tomorrow. If they had to part, he was determined to do his damnedest to make this last day memorable for both of them.

Davis wouldn't be back until evening since Nick had offered to feed him supper as well. He and Vala might not be able to spend the last night together but they had a lot of daylight hours still at their disposal.

She was a beautiful woman, still with that appealing look of fragility she'd had as a girl. She wasn't fragile—far from it. Hadn't she held her own on the trip into the Superstitions? He shook his head, remembering how she'd suffered after her lie to him about being a rider. Yet she'd gone on. One tough lady.

Her eyelids fluttered and opened. He gazed into

her clear blue eyes and found words he didn't mean to say trembling on his lips. With some effort, he held them back and looked away, afraid he might blurt out something he wasn't sure he meant.

"Where's Sheba?" she asked.

"Apparently she decided we weren't doing anything she disapproved of, so she left."

Rising onto an elbow, he brushed a strand of hair from her cheek. "Anyone ever tell you what a sexy woman you are?" he asked.

"What makes you think so?" she asked with a wicked little smile.

"It could have something to do with the fact you're sliding your foot up my leg toward a very sensitive spot. Then again, maybe it's because just looking at you sends me up."

He groaned when her foot made contact with his arousal, and he retaliated by sliding his hand over her thigh to the warmth between her legs.

Though he'd never kept count of how many times he'd made love to a woman in the space of a few hours, he was certain today would surpass any record he might have set. Just as Vala surpassed any other woman he'd ever known. He couldn't get enough of her.

From the eager way she responded, she must feel the same about him. A thrill of pure masculine pride shot through him. She was the only woman in the world he'd ever cared enough about to want to impress any way he could.

As they came together, it was as though this was

the first time he'd made love with her. He wanted her with all the passion and need he'd brought to that night under the penultimate moon.

"You know what?" she murmured as they lay entwined afterward.

"Can't imagine," he said.

"Your bed is more comfortable for lovemaking than your sleeping bag."

"I can see you're getting spoiled."

"Another thing."

"What?"

"I'm hungry."

So was he, now that he thought about it.

Still naked, they finished off what was left of the brunch, then took another dip in the Jacuzzi.

"We could go swimming," he suggested. "Ever tried it nude?"

"Outside? Your house is in the middle of a city, for heaven's sake."

"There's a fence around the backyard."

"But still—"

"Scared?"

"I told you I'm not used to—well, running all over the place naked."

"All the more reason to try swimming that way."

"I thought people weren't supposed to swim right after they ate."

He grinned at her. "We'll stay in the shallow end. Try it, you'll like it."

"Why do I get the feeling that the next thing you'll want me to do is don wild geese feathers so I can fly with you?"

"No need, when we fly together just fine without them."

"I'll bet you were formidable in court," she said. "You're hard to outargue. Okay, one quick swim and, if anyone looks over the fence, you're in real trouble."

Once she was actually outside in the swimming pool, Vala forgot about being naked. Although the water's caress wasn't the same as in the Jacuzzi, she found swimming a totally different experience without a suit on. For good or ill, one by one her inhibitions were dissolving and it was all Bram's doing.

It made her realize how conservative Neal had been. He'd never liked to be caught without clothes on. She wouldn't have dreamed of undressing in front of him.

She smiled, reveling in the freedom of no clothes at all. Being with Bram was unlike anything she'd ever known. With him she was learning to be herself.

Later, wrapped in towels, they lounged in the dappled shade of a Russian olive tree. She noticed he seemed deep in thought.

"Care to share?" she asked.

He turned to look at her. "I'm seriously considering going back, at least part time, to my original profession."

"Oh? Why?"

"Would you believe Mokesh told me I had to get out there and fight?"

She blinked. What on earth was he talking about? "Mokesh?" she repeated.

"Yup. In all his rattler finery, he came to me in a vision-dream. Said if I'm Ndee, then I'd better contribute—or else. I figure as a lawyer I can stir the pot, get it boiling and see what cooks up. I've always looked forward to challenges."

"I can believe that."

"But reality-based Vala is withholding judgment on the vision bit?"

She tried to be as truthful as possible. "Something like that is beyond my experience, but I'm not so narrow-minded as to deny it can exist. However the idea came to you, though, I think what you've decided to do will be good for both you and the Ndee."

He gave her a crooked grin. "Glad to have you in my corner."

She bit back the words that would have told him she'd always be in his corner, no matter what. Instead, she focused on the here and now. "Do you know what time Davis will be back?"

"I've been waiting for you to ask. We don't have to get dressed until five, at the earliest. Nick is treating him to supper. Until then, fair maiden, you're my captive."

"Oh mercy me," she wailed in mock fright, "whatever shall I do? Here I am helpless and un-clad in the clutches of a warrior. And not just any old warrior, but an Apache, as I, in my ignorance call them—the most feared of all warriors."

"You got that right." Bram rose and loomed over her lounge chair. "Do you come peacefully or by force?"

Giggling, in a sudden swift leap, she shot from the chair, eluded his grasp and ran across the back lawn, losing her towel on the way.

He was after her like a shot and she darted this way and that to avoid capture. Both of them naked, they raced over the grass until he lunged and caught her. Lifting her into his arms, he trotted to-ward the back door. As he shifted her to open it, Vala caught a glimpse of a man on the other side of the back fence. He stood on a tall ladder, ap-parently repairing a gutter on his house.

She carried his expression of mixed amazement and amusement with her into the house.

"Your neighbor over the fence saw us!" she cried.

"Bet he's sorry he's not me," Bram told her as he dropped her onto his bed.

This time their lovemaking was slow, so sweet and tender she felt she would never forget this man, this day, this moment. How could she when she knew this would be the last time they'd lie together like this.

Later, after showering, Vala put on her new Arizona clothes, tying her hair back with the scarf.

"You look so different," Bram told her. "I'm not sure we shouldn't stay right here so I can get to know the new you."

"You already know all you need to about me," she told him, pleased at his admiration.

They drove to a nearby Mexican restaurant for an early dinner, arriving back at the house shortly before Nick pulled up with Davis.

"You can park this kid with me anytime," Nick told them. "Man, can he pick winners. Called 'em, six out of eight, damn good odds."

While Davis tried not to look as proud as he felt, Bram explained that the boy had predicted, in six out of the eight bronc riders, which man would stay on his horse and which man would fail to.

Vala smiled. "Heavens, I hope this doesn't mean he'll grow up to be a bookie."

"He did watch the horses, not the riders," Nick said, "so maybe you got something to worry about."

Davis shook his head. "Naw, I'm gonna be a shaman."

Nick's eyebrows rose. "Oho, so that's your secret."

He clapped Davis on the shoulder. "Hope we can get together next time you're in these parts, amigo."

After he left, Davis said, "We had a really awesome time, Nick and me. And, yes, Mom, I re-

membered to thank him. What'd you guys do while
I was gone?"

We had a pretty awesome time ourselves, Vala
thought.

"We went swimming and sort of lay around," she
told him, the understatement of the century.

The phone rang, Bram answered it and came
back with the news that the airline had confirmed
their reservations for noon tomorrow.

Davis muttered, "Bummer."

Silently, Vala echoed him.

FIFTEEN

Vala slept better than she'd expected to, considering it was her last night in Arizona, the last night anywhere near Bram. When she woke in the morning, she lay quietly for a bit, thinking she might be boarding a jet at noon, but she'd be leaving her heart behind. It made no difference how Bram felt about her—she loved him. On this treasure map trip, what she'd found was a man worth loving.

After she showered, she put on the navy pants suit, but wore the bright yellow shirt she'd bought in the mall with it, instead of the plain white one. For some reason, this lightened her spirits a little.

When she went into the kitchen, through the sliding doors she noticed Bram and Davis were standing on the patio in what looked to be earnest conversation. No doubt having to do with how soon Bram can send the kitten, she thought.

Davis glanced her way, saw her, waved and then the two of them, Davis still talking, walked away from the house into the yard.

Vala shrugged and went about fixing herself

breakfast. Though she didn't feel much like eating, the idea of facing airline food for the rest of the day made her decide to eat something decent while she had the chance.

She was downing her second cup of coffee when Davis came through the sliding doors into the kitchen. Bram, she saw, was still in the yard, apparently contemplating one of the grapefruit trees.

"He's thinking things over," Davis informed her.

"I know he's planning some changes in his life," she said.

"You do?" Davis sounded surprised.

"I think he intends to start lawyering for the Ndee. It seems he had a dream where Mokesh told him to."

"Whoa! It was really Mokesh?"

"In his rattlesnake form."

"Awesome. So he's gonna do it?"

Vala nodded. "Your map made a difference in Bram's life, didn't it?"

"Mine, too," Davis said. "And yours."

Startled, she stared at him. "Why do you say in my life?"

"Um—" David tugged at his ear. "Well, you learned to ride a horse, didn't you?"

Not sure he wasn't concealing something, she would have pursued it if Bram hadn't pushed open the sliding door and entered just then. When her gaze fastened on him, everything else fled from her mind.

He looked at her with those wonderful dark eyes and she was caught, unable to move or speak, feeling the arc of emotion flashing between them, filling her heart.

"I have an errand to run before we leave for the airport," he said finally, breaking the spell. "Be back soon."

Bram took the BMW, easing it into the flow of traffic, turning off at the mall, thinking he didn't have much time for what he had to do. He shook his head. Wouldn't be doing it at all if it weren't for Davis. Smart kid. He couldn't say the same for himself.

His mother's favorite word for those unfortunates a can or two short of a sixpack was noodleheads. He'd never believed he belonged there but damned if he hadn't just about joined his mother's noodlehead club.

In the jewelry store, he asked the female clerk, "If you were a no-nonsense lady of maybe sixty, living alone in the Superstitions, but with an eye for beauty, what do you think would catch your eye in here?"

"Does she prefer Native American designs?" the unfazed clerk asked, gesturing toward a tray of turquoise set in silver. In a box next to the tray he saw a gold snake pin with yellow gem eyes and small chips of turquoise set into the body in a diamondback pattern. "Mokesh," he muttered under his breath.

He pointed. "I'll take the snake."

After Pauline got this gift she could no longer claim there wasn't gold in the Superstitions, he thought with amusement. The gold snake, though, was only a token. He owed Pauline more than he could ever repay.

He finished his shopping and drove back to the house. Inside, he found Vala and Davis on the floor by the kitten box. It hadn't taken Sheba long to learn Davis meant her kittens no harm and, though she made her usual mother noises, she didn't object to the boy holding Zorro.

Davis had the kitten snugged up against his face while Vala watched, smiling.

"I'd say Zorro is the luckiest one of the lot," Bram said to them. "Kinked tail, crossed eyes and all."

"I hope he won't mind New York winters," Vala said.

"Not to worry." When she glanced up at him, he added, "Cats are adaptable."

"I whispered to him so he wouldn't miss me too much," Davis said. "I told him we'd be together soon."

Vala rose and, leaving Davis with the kitten, followed Bram into the living room.

"All packed?" he asked.

She nodded.

"I like that yellow shirt," he said. "You look good in bright colors."

Hell, to him she looked good in anything. Or nothing. But the colors she'd worn before she bought that skirt and this shirt in the mall here tended to be dark ones. Or plain white. In his mind the brighter shades meant she'd come out of her shell. It gave him a thrill to think that at least part of that was his doing.

"Thank you," she told him.

He took a jewelry box from his pocket, saying, "I want to show you the pin I bought for Pauline."

When Vala gazed at the pin, she murmured, "Mokesh. Perfect."

"Will you help me gift wrap it before we take off for the airport? They'd have done it at the jewelry store but I wanted you to see it."

"I mean to send her something from Davis and me, too," she said. "I thought maybe a wool shawl. I've seen some colorful ones in the stores back home."

"Sounds like something she could use. Send the shawl to me and I'll see she gets it."

He watched Vala's deftness with admiration as she wrapped the box in the gold paper he'd bought and affixed the gold elastic bow.

"I made some cheese sandwiches to bring with us on the plane," she said, "in case the food turns out to be as bad as it usually is."

"Good idea. Someday someone's going to make a mint putting up box lunches to take aboard. My favorite would be smoked salmon, homemade brown bread with a cream cheese spread and an apple turnover."

She smiled. "Pricey, but delicious, I'll admit."

He could tell her smile was forced and he longed to wrap his arms around her and never let her go.

But if he touched her, he was none too sure what might happen.

"I'll load the bags into the car," he said.

Vala watched him go out. So far she'd managed to act in a reasonably adult manner and she hoped she could keep it up at least until she was aboard the jet. Davis would be feeling bad, too, so he shouldn't be too upset to see her cry.

Her son, though, seemed to be taking this departure far better than she. He actually seemed to be more excited than sad. Come to think of it, he had enjoyed the flight here—his first—and so maybe he was anticipating being on the jet, even though he didn't want to leave Arizona. He also had something to look forward to in a few weeks when the kitten arrived.

She had nothing.

Damn it, why was she going away from Bram without ever telling him how she felt? What was the harm in admitting her love for him now that he didn't have to feel embarrassed about not reciprocating? She nodded. At the last minute, just before she had to get on the plane, she'd tell him. Whisper it in his ear along with her goodbye.

She took a deep breath and let it out slowly, feeling not quite so depressed.

There was the usual traffic at the airport, the hassle of parking and getting a redcap to check the bags she and Davis weren't carrying on, but Bram handled it all with speed and dispatch. She should have known he would. He handled everything well.

They were in good time, but not so early as to have to stand around too long. No glitches occurred—quite the contrary. At the airline counter they honored her return tickets, upgrading them to first class, confirmed the noon departure and even offered an apology for the delay.

Finally, they arrived at the gate. She'd thought maybe they wouldn't let Bram through, but that didn't happen. He set down her carry-on bag and took her hands in his.

"I wish we could avoid being apart," he said.

So did she, but found she couldn't say so even after swallowing to try to rid herself of the lump in her throat. She was vaguely conscious that Davis had moved a ways off, though still keeping an eye on them, but that didn't matter. Nothing mattered except having to leave Bram.

"I have a secret to tell you." Bram's voice seemed to come from a long way off and it took her a minute to understand what he was saying.

"A secret?" she mumbled.

Ignoring the people around them he leaned closer and whispered into her ear. "This is my secret, that only you know. I love you. Will you come back and marry me?"

Stunned, Vala repeated his words in her mind, hardly believing she'd heard right.

He loved her.

"I—I love you, too," she stammered in a half-whisper, barely able to speak.

"Does that mean you'll marry me?" His warm breath stirred her hair as he whispered the words into her ear.

She clung to him, scarcely able to breathe, and raised up so he could hear her whisper, "Oh, yes. Heavens, yes."

Bram held her away, grinning at her.

She smiled back, happiness surging through her.

And then he kissed her. The world went away, she was conscious of nothing but Bram until someone tugged at her jacket and Davis's voice said, "Mom, they're announcing that the first-class passengers can board now. That's us."

Bram let her go, enveloped Davis in a bear hug and thrust a small velvet box into her hand. In a blur of movement she somehow got aboard the jet with Davis, found the right seat and got her bag stowed.

"What did he give you?" Davis asked.

She looked down at the red velvet box she was holding and slowly, carefully pried up the lid. A diamond set in the center of a cluster of sapphires winked up at her.

"Whoa, that's a way cool ring, Mom. You gonna put it on?"

As she slid the ring onto her left fourth finger, discovering it fit perfectly, reason began to return. This was an engagement ring. She was going to marry Bram. And she was going to have to explain this to Davis. After a moment's thought, she decided a blunt statement was the way to go.

The attendant came by and reminded her to fasten her seat belt. Noting that Davis already had his on, she buckled hers, then turned to him.

He spoke before she could begin. "So, how soon are you guys gonna get married?"

Vala gaped at him. "I didn't think you could possibly have overheard us in the waiting room," she said finally.

Davis grinned. "I didn't."

"Then how—?"

"You know when Bram and me took a walk in the backyard this morning? What I did was tell him the end of the Wind Dancer story—the one Pauline told me. That's what she said I had to do before we left Arizona."

Vala recalled that before they left Pauline's cabin, the old woman had taken Davis aside to tell him something and he'd promised he wouldn't forget.

"Pauline said you two needed a push to reach the right decision and that I was the one who had to do it. She'd already told me all of the Wind Dancer story, so I knew how it ended, but you guys didn't 'cause I wasn't supposed to let on till I could tell that you needed a push. Mostly Bram, 'cause the man's supposed to do the asking."

Vala shook her head in amazement. "Do I get to hear the end of that story?"

"Sure. Wind Dancer, changed into Hummingbird, whispered secret love words in his bride's ear. On account of that, the Ndee believe a man who loves a woman and wants to marry her has to whisper a secret in her ear or else she won't ever be his bride. That's what I told Bram this morning. He's Ndee, so he understood. And it's a good thing I did what Pauline said, otherwise you guys never would have gotten around to it."

Unsuccessfully blinking back tears, Vala leaned over and kissed her son on the cheek.

"Hey, you're not supposed to cry; you're supposed to be happy," he said.

"Sometimes people cry when they're very, very happy," she told him. "Like me right now."

"That's good then. 'Cause I'm happy, too. Bram likes me as much as he does you, except in a different way. He told me that this morning. He said getting me as his son would be the best wedding present in the world."

Davis's beaming smile made Vala's tears flow faster.

The attendant, passing by, asked if she was all right.

Tears running down her cheeks, unable to speak, Vala held out her left hand to show her engagement ring.

"My mom's okay," Davis said. "She's crying 'cause she's happy. I guess it's one of the things I got to learn about women."

EPILOGUE

A year later, in Arizona, Vala and Bram were curled up together on the couch in the living room one evening, watching Zorro attack his mother's tail and making bets as to how soon Sheba would give him a smack.

"She's got more patience than I have," Vala said.

Bram didn't answer and she saw that he had his head cocked to one side, as if listening.

"What's wrong?" she asked. "Do you hear the baby?" Their daughter had been born prematurely and, though she was thriving now, Vala couldn't help worrying about her.

"Nope. Sounds to me like Davis is talking to someone."

Listening, Vala heard a low singsong. "It's more like he's telling a story. But who to?"

They looked at one another and nodded, rose and headed for the nursery, making no noise with their bare feet.

Three-month-old Letty Hunter lay in her bassinet, her dark eyes fixed on Davis who was standing beside it, telling his baby sister a story.

"And so Quo-Qui, the littlest boy of the Ndee, the one they'd always laughed at, saved his people by his cleverness," he finished. Reaching into the bassinet, he touched Letty's hand and she curled hers around his forefinger.

"I like you, too," Davis said softly. "It doesn't matter that you got born too soon and so you're really, really tiny. That's why I told you about Quo-Qui, so you'd hear something good about being small. I'm your big brother and I'll always take care of you."

Letty made a tiny sound, more a squeak than anything else.

"Pretty soon you'll get bigger and then I'll take you for rides in your stroller," he went on. "Maybe I can show you a roadrunner, then, 'cause that's what Quo-Qui changed into. But even if you never do get real big, you don't need to worry about being small. Like the story says, the littlest will triumph in the end. Just ask me. *I* know."

Bram and Vala glanced at one another and she saw the tears in her eyes were reflected in his. They tiptoed away and embraced in the hall, holding tightly to each other. Love might not cure all ills, but it lit up every moment of their lives as brightly as the Arizona sun.

BOOK YOUR PLACE ON OUR WEBSITE
AND MAKE THE
READING CONNECTION!

We've created a customized website just for our very special readers, where you can get the inside scoop on everything that's going on with Zebra, Pinnacle and Kensington books.

When you come online, you'll have the exciting opportunity to:

- View covers of upcoming books

- Read sample chapters

- Learn about our future publishing schedule (listed by publication month *and author*)

- Find out when your favorite authors will be visiting a city near you

- Search for and order backlist books from our online catalog

- Check out author bios and background information

- Send e-mail to your favorite authors

- Meet the Kensington staff online

- Join us in weekly chats with authors, readers and other guests

- Get writing guidelines

- AND MUCH MORE!

Visit our website at
http://www.zebrabooks.com

COMING IN JANUARY FROM
ZEBRA BOUQUET ROMANCES

#29 SAND CASTLES by Kate Holmes
__(0-8217-6457-8, $3.99) Artist Alys Vincent never expected to fall in love with the sun-bronzed hunk she'd approached on the beach to model for her. But when she found herself in Jerod's strong arms, she dared to dream that they could build a love more enduring than golden summer days . . . and sand castles.

#30 BENEATH A TEXAS MOON by Clara Wimberly
__(0-8217-6458-6, $3.99) Jessica McLean's girlhood crush on Diego Serrat had turned into grown-up passion—until he left her with a broken heart and a precious secret. Now, the tough Texas Ranger is back in town on assignment. His job—to protect her. But who will protect Jessica's heart?

#31 DANGEROUS MOVES by Mary Morgan
__(0-8217-6459-4, $3.99) Rodeo star Dillon McRay has lived his life on the principle that you only go around once. Now, he's determined to make the most of it—with beautiful Brooke Stephenson. Although she believes she's not the gambling type, Dillon's got to convince her that some chances are worth taking.

#32 A MATTER OF TRUST by Deb Stover
__(0-8217-6460-8, $3.99) Every man has a woman he can't forget, and for sexy veterinarian Gordon Lane, that woman is Taylor Bowen . . . back in Digby, Colorado, and more beautiful than ever. Can he and Taylor find the courage to reclaim an old love?

Call toll free **1-888-345-BOOK** to order by phone or use this coupon to order by mail.

Name_____

Address_____

City_____ State _____ Zip _____

Please send me the books I have checked above.

I am enclosing $_____
Plus postage and handling* $_____
Sales tax (in NY and TN) $_____
Total amount enclosed $_____

*Add $2.50 for the first book and $.50 for each additional book.

Send check or Money order (no cash or CODs) to:

Kensington Publishing Corp., 850 Third Avenue, New York, NY 10022

Prices and Numbers subject to change without notice. Valid only in the U.S.

All Books will be available 1/1/00. All orders subject to availability.

Check out our web site at **www.kensingtonbooks.com**